Aunt Matilda's Ghost

For Ben, Lillian and Frances with best wishes for happy reading!
Mignon F. Ballard

Mignon Franklin Ballard

SILVER DAGGER
M Y S T E R I E S

Hardcover ISBN 1-57072-116-5
Trade Paper ISBN 1-57072-132-7
Originally published in 1978 by Aurora Publishers, Inc.
Reprinted in 2000 by The Overmountain Press
Copyright © 2000 by Mignon Franklin Ballard
Printed in the United States of America
All Rights Reserved

1 2 3 4 5 6 7 8 9 0

For Gene

FOREWORD

On June 2, 1857, Dr. Alexander Means successfully demonstrated in Atlanta, Georgia, what may have been the world's first incandescent light. At that time a professor of chemistry at both Atlanta Medical College and Emory College, Dr. Means later became Emory's fourth president.

The electrical machine is now on display at Emory College in Oxford, Georgia.

The character of Dr. Joseph Summerville in this book is based on that of Dr. Means. All other characters are entirely fictitious.

M.F.B.

PROLOGUE

"What did you do for fun when you were a little girl growing up in King's Creek?" I asked my mom. "It must've been really boring."

Mom just smiled. "King's Creek is much larger now, and I guess there are more things to do, but we were never bored. I can't believe it's been over twenty years since we first came to live in the house at Walnut Hill. What an exciting summer that was! Something was happening every minute, it seemed."

"Like what?" I asked.

"Like meeting Aunt Matilda," she said with a secret kind of smile.

"Aunt Matilda? Who's she?"

"Why don't I make us a pitcher of lemonade? We'll take it out on the porch where it's cool, and I'll tell you all about it."

And so she did. My mom's name then was Peggy Patrick, and this is her story.

CHAPTER 1

I still get kind of shivery when I think about Aunt Matilda. Maybe you don't believe in ghosts. Well, neither did I, but that was before we came to live here at Walnut Hill, before we met Aunt Matilda.

I wasn't especially happy about moving to Walnut Hill, not even when Danny told me it was haunted. People had seen lights, she claimed, and heard noises and spooky stuff like that.

"Bosh!" I had said, but not for long.

Danny is my Grandmother Summerville, and everyone says she doesn't look like a grandmother at all, but she acts like one sometimes. When I was just beginning to talk, my daddy paid me a quarter to call her "Granny" just to see what she would do, but I couldn't say "Granny," so it came out "Danny." That suited my grandmother fine. Now my brother, Robert, calls her that too, but I was the one who started it.

Walnut Hill is a big, old, white house in a little college town, and my Grandfather Summerville was born here. So was his father and his grandfather too. Mama says that my Great-Great-Great-Grandfather Summerville built the house way back in the 1830s when he was president of the little college here.

The house could be pretty, I guess, if the inside were fixed up more. The outside looks okay now with a fresh coat of paint and those four tall columns in front. But there's something different about this house—besides being old, I mean—and I guess I knew it then. I just didn't know what it was.

I'll never forget the first time we went inside after Mama bought the house from her cousin Thomas. It looked awful! The floors rolled so that if you put a marble down, it would be on the other side of the room before you could stand up straight again. The floorboards were about a foot wide and were painted an icky brown; but worse than that, the bathtubs sat on legs! Mama thought they were quaint. You would have thought we were moving into the White House the way she carried on.

The day we moved in I didn't even want to go inside. I sat on the front steps and sulked, hoping I was getting in everyone's way. I was really in a nasty mood. Danny thought so too.

"Get up off those steps, Peggy Patrick!" she demanded. "You've pouted long enough." Danny doesn't have a world of patience.

Well, I mumbled and grumbled and skulked around a little, but I knew it wouldn't do me any good, so I started dragging all my junk upstairs to my room. It was a big room done in a soft shade of yellow with four large windows, and even a window seat. "A room to grow in," Danny had said. Maybe it was, but I didn't care.

We worked all morning unloading our assorted belongings from the van. Mama had hired two men to move the heavy stuff, but she was paying them by the hour, so we had to hurry things along. Once when I was walking back to the truck, the girl from across the street rode by on her bike and waved. I didn't wave back.

To make matters worse, my locomotive brother crashed into me on the stairs just before I reached the landing with my last load of books. Books flew everywhere, but mostly on my bare feet!

"Did you have to make me break my foot?" I yelled.

Rob's face looked like he had dipped it in milk, freckles and all. "I thought I saw somebody up there."

I looked at the trail of books on the stairs and rubbed my foot. "I sure wish it had been me."

Rob didn't smile. "I'm not kidding. Maybe it's the way the light comes in that window over the landing, but for a minute I thought I saw a lady standing there."

"Huh, you don't scare me, Robert Patrick. You just weren't looking where you were going—as usual."

He didn't answer, but he did help me pick up my books. He had two mysterious shopping bags full of clanky things. It didn't take much of a genius to know he didn't want me to see in them.

I was determined to see in them. "What's in the bags, the family jewels?" I made a grab and missed.

He clattered out of my reach and disappeared into his room at the end of the wide hall. "Stay away!" he threatened, slamming the door.

"What's going on out here?" Danny stuck her head out of the room next to mine. "Can't you two get along for today at least?"

With her short curls hidden under a dusty scarf, and her smooth, manicured nails covered by working gloves, she looked almost like a grandmother should, even to the smudge of dirt on her chin. I shrugged. "He makes such a big deal about his old inventions! Who cares?"

Danny laughed. "You care! Come on in here a minute. Some of your things are mixed in with mine."

I shuffled after her and sank down on her cluttered bed while she began to unload her "magic potions." That's what Danny calls cosmetics.

"I've been up and down those stairs a dozen times today and we're still not through," I griped. "I'm tired."

Danny tossed aside a crumpled tube of toothpaste and an empty cold-cream jar. "I think the truck's about empty now. Find something else to do for a while. Meet some of the neighbors. What about that little blonde girl across the street?"

"Lucy?" I slid into a heap on the floor. "She's prissy. She runs with her hands in the air. Besides, all she knows how to do is cheer."

Danny turned her back, but I knew she was smiling. "A lot of girls like to cheer, Peggy. You might like it, too."

I licked my finger and washed a clean circle in the middle of my dirty knee. "I have other things to do," I said. My knees looked awful and so did the rest of me. "I wish we had never come to this old place," I grumbled, staring at a piece of cracked plaster on the big high ceiling. "The whole house is going to fall on our heads."

I wanted somebody to comfort me, and Danny did, in her way. "I think somebody's making a fuss for the sake of making a fuss," she said, stooping beside me. "I thought you wanted to come and live here at Walnut Hill. Just think of all the history around you! Imagine all the people who have lived in these rooms. Why, you might even meet a ghost! It's supposed to have one, you know."

"Really, Danny!" I snorted. "I'm twelve years old now, remember? Besides, Mama's the only one who really wanted to move. I liked it where we were."

Danny pulled off her gloves slowly, one finger at a time. "I want you to promise me one thing, Margaret."

I squirmed. When Danny calls me "Margaret," it usually means I am going to have to do something I don't like. But I agreed; after all, what could be worse than moving to this weird old house?

"Promise me that you won't let your mother know how you feel." Danny stared straight into my eyes. "Your mother has wanted to live in this house since she heard stories about it as a child. It's like coming home to her, and it means something special. I don't want you to ruin it."

I wasn't ready to give up. "But her dress shop, Danny—it was doing okay where we were. Now she'll have to start all over again."

Danny nodded. "I know, but she and I will worry about that part. You concentrate on your problem: you're here now, and that's that. So make the best of it."

I looked at all the confusion around us. "But why?" I groaned.

"I'll tell you why." Danny tucked the hair back in one of my braids. "Your mother has had to raise you two alone since your father died, except for the help I give her. Living here in King's Creek will make it a little easier. You don't remember much about your father, Peggy, but he would have liked it here, too. This is his kind of place." She smiled. "Won't you give it a try?"

My eyes felt hot and I swallowed a big lump in my throat. It was terrible being so mean and selfish, and even worse knowing I would get over feeling sorry in a little while and start being mean and selfish all over again. With luck, maybe I'll improve with age.

Danny absently patted my arm. I knew she was trying to think of a comforting cliché to make me feel better. Danny carries a battered box of dusty expressions in her mind, and if she thinks the occasion calls for it, she can whip one out in a minute. Her eyes brightened and I knew she had dug up just the right one for me.

"Just remember," Danny said, "every cloud has a silver lining. It's always darkest before the dawn."

I was doubly blest.

CHAPTER 2

I had a hard time going to sleep that night. My eyes ached from staring at bare walls and blank, curtainless windows, and my stomach ached because my eyes ached. I wanted to wake up and be in my old room back home. I could picture the dotted swiss curtains, the crazy wallpaper, the dogwood tree outside my window. They swam in a hot haze behind my eyes. I knew what homesick was.

In the night something woke me. It was the smell, I think— a peculiar smell like forgotten flowers left too long in a vase. *Maybe all old houses smell like this*, I thought, sniffing. Then I reached for the tissue beside my bed and discovered that my face was wet; my pillow was wet. I had been crying in my sleep.

In the morning the smell was gone.

The kitchen was hopeless. Mama said that at least half of all household goods go into the kitchen, and ours were still in packing boxes in the middle of the floor. Robert and I ate cereal on the back steps, staring into the woods behind our house. They looked interesting. I wanted to check them out, but there was too much unpacking to do and I was still sleepy. I yawned.

My brother slurped up a mouthful of cornflakes and grinned. "What's the matter? Didn't you sleep last night?"

"Of course I did," I lied. "Don't talk with your mouth full."

He squinted at me, still chewing. "Hey, you didn't see anything last night, did you?"

"See anything? Oh, you mean like ghosts and stuff? Nope, sorry. I didn't even see your lady on the stairs."

He stood up so he would be taller than I was. "I didn't say it *was* a lady. I said that it *looked* like a lady!"

I laughed. "Surely you don't believe that tale about ghosts, Rob. Even a ten-year-old should know the difference between real and make-believe."

He sat down again. "What tale? Did Danny tell you about it?"

"She just said that this house is supposed to have a ghost," I said. "You don't have to worry. I don't know anything you don't know."

"I know you don't," he gloated. "If you did, you'd know this ghost couldn't be a lady. Our ghost is a man!"

"Who told you that?" I crowed.

"It's just something I heard Danny telling Mama about last night. You really don't know about it, do you?" He looked pleased with himself.

"If I did, would I ask you?" I was losing my patience.

He stared at me for a minute, trying to decide if he should keep his secret a little longer or blurt it all out. He blurted. I knew he would; he always does.

"Well," he began, counting on his fingers, "it's supposed to be Great-Great-Great-Grandfather Summerville's ghost."

"Ah-ha!" (Rob hates it when I say "ah-ha!") "I knew you'd tell me sooner or later."

He looked peeved. "You still don't know everything. Maybe ten-year-olds aren't so dumb after all."

"What's to know?" I got up to put my bowl in the kitchen.

"Oh come on, Peggy. Didn't you really know about the ghost? Great-Great-Great-Grandfather Summerville was a scientist, you know, and an inventor, too. They say he comes back to work on his inventions."

"I knew he was an inventor. I just didn't know he was a

ghost."

"Well, he was, and I'm going to be one, too!" Rob gulped at his mistake. "An inventor, I mean—not a ghost."

"Well, if we have to have a ghost," I said, "I hope it's one who groans and moans and floats around in the middle of the night. I don't understand the friendly variety."

Rob looked uncomfortable. "I think this one does the 'footstep and flash of light' kind of thing."

"Really?" Things were beginning to look a little brighter in this old museum of a house. I grabbed his hand and started for the back door. "Come on! Let's find out what this ghost is all about."

We found Mama in the kitchen, scrubbing the inside of the big wooden cabinets. Only her feet were showing; the rest of her had disappeared in the dark hole under the sink.

"Hey, Mama!" I called, trying to keep from stumbling over all the cartons on the floor. "Why didn't you tell me this house had a ghost?"

"Don't bother me about ghosts now," a hollow voice grumbled from under the counter. Mama backed into view and wiped her forehead with the back of her hand. "I hope we never move again!"

She rested her head against the cabinet door. "Just look at all of these dishes I have to put away. And you want to hear ghost stories."

"Why, Peggy Patrick! I thought you were too sophisticated to believe in ghosts." Danny stood laughing in the doorway.

I grinned, feeling the red creep into my face. "Do you really believe in them, Danny?"

She sank down on a plump-looking box marked "dish towels, aprons, and pot holders" and crossed her legs neatly. "Only on Halloween," she answered. "But your Grandfather Summerville did. Both he and your Uncle Zeb claimed to have seen or heard something while they were living here."

"Robert saw it, too," I jeered. "Right out there on the stairs!"

Rob's face turned the color of a strawberry milk shake.

He gave me a dirty look. "I remember Uncle Zeb," he said to Danny. "He lived in this house for a long time, didn't he?"

Danny was searching the refrigerator for her skim milk. "Of course you remember him," she said. "Uncle Zeb was really your great-uncle, your grandfather's brother. He and Aunt Jane were Thomas's parents, and when they died, they left the house to Thomas. He sold it to us."

"Aunt Jane and Uncle Zeb lived here as long as I can remember," Mama told us. She poured cold apple juice into paper cups. "When you were little, we used to come and see them. Remember?"

"Just barely," I said, waiting thirstily for my juice. I took a long cool swallow. "Wasn't Uncle Zeb a doctor?"

"He practiced medicine for nearly fifty years," said Mama, who seemed glad of a chance to rest. "His office was where our playroom is. He was a plump, cheerful old gentleman: reminded me of Santa Claus when I was a little girl."

Danny laughed. "Your Uncle Zeb would have called himself portly, not plump; but he did love children. It's a shame he and Jane never had but the one son."

"I guess he was so busy with the patients in this town, he considered them all his children," Mama answered. "Anyway, I'm glad Thomas decided to live in Atlanta instead of here in King's Creek, or he never would have sold us this house." Mama looked relieved.

"He's lived away too long to want to come back now," Danny reminded her. "I think he was glad to have some of the family take the house off his hands."

"Maybe that's because of the ghost," Rob said.

"Tell us about the ghost . . . please, Danny?" I flashed my most adorable smile. It wasn't much, but it was the best I could do.

Danny wasn't taken easily. "Only if you promise to pitch in and help with the unpacking. Rome wasn't built in a day, you know."

I didn't even make a face. "I know, Danny, and we will, I promise; but if we're going to live with a ghost, shouldn't we know something about it?"

Ancestors are a complicated bunch. I was trying to get mine straightened out in my head. "Let's see, now, there was Uncle Zeb and my grandfather, John. Were there only the two brothers?"

"No, there was a girl, too," Danny answered. "But she died rather young, I think. At least she never married."

"Aunt Matilda," Mama murmured in a thoughtful voice. "I remember Daddy mentioning her. Uncle Zeb was the oldest, then Aunt Matilda, and finally John: my father and your grandfather. He died before you were born."

Rob frowned. "Golly, families are confusing! All those aunts and uncles and great-this and great-that. It's too much like history for me."

"Do you suppose this house really is haunted?" I was beginning to worry a little. "I've heard of people who had to leave home because ghosts wouldn't leave them alone."

"Don't be so serious, Peggy," Mama laughed. "It's only a story. Besides, your Uncle Zeb managed to live here quite happily."

I was a little disappointed. "You mean nobody has really seen the ghost?"

"Oh, some claim to have seen strange lights at night, and others have heard footsteps," Mama said. "People like to think it's the ghost of your Great-Great-Great-Grandfather Summerville looking for his invention."

Rob swallowed loudly. "Now, that's what I want to hear about!"

"Danny can tell you more about that," Mama explained. "You see, my father—your Grandfather Summerville—was raised in this old house; he grew up hearing these tales. I only remember a little."

"What kind of invention was it?" Rob wanted to know.

"Your grandfather told me it was a forerunner of the modern-day electric light," Danny said. "The story is that sometime in 1857, when Thomas Edison was only a boy, your Great-Great-Great-Grandfather Summerville demonstrated the first incandescent light."

"Gosh!" Rob was wide-eyed. "What happened then? Where is it now?"

Danny shook her head. "I wish I knew. The evidence was documented that such a demonstration was made, but we never knew what happened to the actual invention. It just disappeared."

Rob had gotten red in the face. He looked like a firecracker about to explode. "You mean it's gone? The invention is gone?"

"Maybe there never was one," I said, disappointed. "Maybe he never really invented it."

"Well, of course he did!" Danny was indignant. "Your ancestor was a well-known scientist; he even worked with Michael Faraday. And the demonstration was successful. There's a write-up about it somewhere or other. It's just that nobody knows what happened to the invention."

"Wouldn't it be great if we could find it?" Rob whooped.

I was thinking. "I'll bet the ghost wants us to find it. That's usually why they hang around in the first place, isn't it? They always have some problem or other."

Danny had started to take another swallow of milk, but she laughed instead. "I should think it would be problem enough just being a ghost," she said.

CHAPTER 3

I decided I would like Lucy Parrish a lot better if she looked less like Cinderella without the soot. If a handsome prince suddenly galloped up with a glass slipper, I'm sure Lucy would have the foot to fit it.

We were sitting on the front steps the next morning—Lucy, Rob, and me, and Lucy's gray kitten, Rover. (I asked her why she had named a cat Rover, but all she said was, "Why not?" After all, it's her cat!)

Lucy had straight yellow hair that fell across her cheek in the sun. She was pretty and she smiled a lot. She didn't wear glasses or have freckles; I did. I guess if I looked like Lucy, I'd smile a lot too.

She turned as I was staring at her, and I don't suppose I was thinking very nice thoughts. "What's the matter?" asked Lucy.

I pretended to be studying the kitten on her lap. I hope she never finds out what I was thinking.

"Say, your grandmother told me you had your own newspaper," she went on happily. "I wish you'd let me help you with it sometime. I can draw cartoons."

I was going to tell her that I didn't need any cartoons, but it's hard to be nasty when somebody's smiling at you that way.

"Of course you'll have to tell me what to do," she added, still watching my face. "I wouldn't know where to begin."

I started liking her a little better then. Telling people what to do is right up my alley. Mama says I have leadership abilities. Danny says I'm bossy.

I shrugged. "We can start one today if you want to. There's nothing else to do around here."

Lucy unhooked a thread of her skirt from the kitten's tiny claws and placed her on the step. "What do you think you'll write about?" she asked.

"Oh, lots of things." I watched Rover bounce from step to step. "I might do a feature on your kitten. Most readers like animal stories."

"Just think," Rob reminded me, "if we could find that missing invention, you'd really have something to write about!"

Lucy listened while I told her about the long-lost electrical apparatus, her blue eyes getting wider and wider.

"And that's not all," I added proudly. "There's a ghost too. Danny said my grandfather *saw* it!"

Lucy was not impressed. "Yeah, everybody knows about that, but *I've* never seen it." She moved into the shade of the tall porch column. "Your grandmother lives here too, doesn't she?"

Rob nodded. "Yeah, Mama says if it weren't for me, this would be 'No Man's Land.' Our daddy was killed in an accident when I was a baby, so Danny came to help with us."

"Mama runs a dress shop," I explained to Lucy, "and Danny looks after the house and us."

Lucy looked interested. "Wow, I wish my grandmother lived with us. She always brings me presents when she comes. I'll bet you have a lot of neat clothes with your mother running a dress shop. You can have a new dress anytime you want one, can't you?"

I made a face. "Are you kidding? I wouldn't be caught dead in a dress except on Sunday! Why, I don't have but three, and Mama says she has to chloroform me to make me wear them."

Lucy looked down at her blue-and-white-checkered play-
suit with the gathered skirt. "You must think I'm an awful
sissy."

"Well, there are sissies and there *sissies*," I said reluc-
tantly. "You're one of the better kind."

Rob scrambled to his feet. "Come on! Let's do something,"
he begged. "I'm tired of sittin'."

"Have you seen the old summerhouse yet?" Lucy asked.
"It's a great place to explore."

I jumped to the ground. "I didn't even know there was one.
Where is it?"

"In those woods behind your place. It's way back there.
You can't see it from here."

We started across the backyard where the tall grass was
dry and dusty. "What a funny place to build a summerhouse," I said. "Wonder why they put it so far from the
house?"

"Oh, there used to be a pond back there," Lucy explained.
"But it dried up a long time ago, my mother said. There's an
old toolshed, too, but I don't think it's been used for ages."

"How far back does our land go?" Rob asked as we picked
our way through the brambles.

Lucy didn't stop. "As far as you can see trees. There are
some on the other side of the summerhouse. I think it used
to be an orchard."

We followed in Lucy's brown-sandaled footsteps and
nobody spoke for a while. There were only a few weeks left
in August and soon school would start, but I felt like summer
was just beginning. The woods were cool and green and mysterious. There's a special magic about a quiet, shady place
to me. Maybe it's because the trees are so much older and
taller than I am, but I keep expecting something exciting to
happen: something different and wonderful that has never
happened before.

There were little rustling, woodsy noises around us and
the louder crackle of my clumsy brother plowing through

the bushes.

"Here it is," Lucy said finally. We poked through a clump of foliage and stepped into a sort of clearing.

The summerhouse sat on a low hump of a hill, looking kind of lonesome and sad. Giant oaks pressed in the gaps of its broken latticework sides, and wisteria vines draped about the circular roof as if they meant to shut out the world.

What a perfect secret place, I was thinking. I could tell that Lucy was thinking the same thing. She grinned. "Well, what do you think?"

"Hey, this is not bad!" Rob shouted, tramping up the sagging, wooden steps. "Look, it's round—like a skating rink!"

"Watch out!" Lucy warned him. "Some of those boards are rotten. The only place you'd skate around here is through the floor!"

I agreed. The old plank platform was a little shaky, but the ceiling seemed to be in one piece. This would be a perfect place for my newspaper office, I decided, and told the others so.

But Rob had other ideas. "Well, I just might want to use it myself! But I don't guess you thought about that, did you?"

I hadn't, of course. "I claimed it first," I said. "Besides, why on earth would you want it?"

"For my inventions, you dummy! This has all the room I'll need."

I was about to slug him when Lucy's eyes caught my attention. She was looking at the old shed on the other side of the summerhouse. "Hey, what about that?" she said. The old shack was dirty and weathered, and its one window had a broken pane, but Lucy looked at it as if it were a palace or something.

When we went over to investigate I saw that it had one sagging shelf and a dirt floor, and that was all. "Ohhh, this is really neat," I crooned, nudging Lucy with my elbow. "Once we get it cleaned up, you could almost live in here!" The idea was so ridiculous, I had to bite my lips to keep from laughing.

Lucy grabbed the ancient door to keep it from falling over.

"And think of the privacy you'd have."

Rob was looking at us suspiciously. For some reason he doesn't trust girls much. But I think he was about to give in when we heard a noise in the bushes somewhere behind us.

Lucy stiffened and motioned for us to be quiet. "I think somebody's out there!" She stared through the jagged window and we crowded against a wall meshed with spiderwebs to look over her shoulder. There was no one in sight. Still I shivered; I had felt a little funny the whole time we had been in the woods. There was a strange feeling about the place.

"Let's get out of here," Rob groaned, stepping on my foot on his way to the door. I was close behind him as we stumbled into the open. There was nobody there—at least not anybody we could see—but I felt like someone was watching every move we made. We would have to find our way back to the house the way we had come and I was in a hurry.

The three of us picked our way through the open spaces. If there had ever been a path from the summerhouse, it had disappeared long ago. It seemed to be taking us twice as long to go back the way we had come. Nobody said much; we were too scared. Even the woods were still. It was quiet, like a cemetery is quiet, and I didn't like it.

CHAPTER 4

Then we saw the note—or at least Lucy did. It was wedged in the split trunk of a cedar tree, and I don't think any of us would have noticed it if the path hadn't been blocked with an X.

We were almost home when I ran into it, and I mean, really ran into it! My toe will never be the same.

I yelled a lot at first. I'm not one to be quiet about pain. "This wasn't here a while ago," I said, holding my aching foot. "Are you sure we're going the right way?"

Lucy was examining the guilty X, which was formed by crossing two pine logs. "I know we did. Don't you remember this tree?"

That was when she spied the paper sticking from its trunk. "Hey, what's this? Looks like a note or something."

I forgot about my toe. "Let me see!"

If you want to solve this mystery,
Follow the trail and you will see
A big surprise; it's just for you!
The signs will tell you what to do.

I reckoned that the writer would rate about a C in penmanship, but the verse was not bad. At the bottom were some funny-looking drawings which were supposed to help us read the signs. They looked like this:

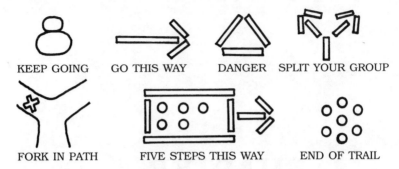

Suddenly I wasn't so scared anymore.

"I know what this is!" Lucy yelled. "It's an Indian trail. We did it in Scouts some."

I was still studying the note. "We've done this at camp too, but I always forget what the signs mean. I'm glad we have something to go by."

Rob swallowed. He looked kind of worried. "What do you mean, Indian trail? You don't mean we're trailing an Indian, do you?"

"No, silly! It's a sort of a game we play in Scouts. Somebody lays a trail using these signs, and another group tries to follow."

He looked relieved. "Sounds like fun! Who do you think laid this one?"

"I don't know." I looked behind us. "Whoever it was is gone now."

"Well, at least it wasn't a ghost," Lucy said. "I was beginning to think this place really is spooked."

"Our ghost only haunts relatives," I laughed. I was beginning to feel almost brave. Whoever laid the trail had done it while we were at the summerhouse. That explained why I had felt like we were being watched.

The trail was easy. Lucy went first because her eyes are better than mine and Rob was still scared. We wound around a while following arrows and rocks until we came to the stick triangle, which meant danger. I gulped, thinking of quick-sand and poisonous snakes, moldy mummies, or vampires with bloody fangs. Then Lucy pointed to a clump of poison ivy trailing up a tree. "There's our danger," she said. I should have known vampires don't come out in the daytime!

Once, we came across the two little arrows which tell you to split your group, but we didn't do it. Nobody wanted to go alone, least of all me. We almost missed the next clue because of all the pine needles on the ground, but Lucy's sharp eyes caught it just before I put my big foot in the middle of a message. Whoever had laid the trail had used pine cones instead of rocks to tell us to take eight steps to the right. We found another note.

> *It cries and yet it's just a tree,*
> *Look in the branches: soon you'll see.*

The words were scrawled in pencil on a piece of notebook paper, just like the first note.

Rob frowned at the paper. "'It cries and yet it's just a tree' . . . what does that mean?"

"Use your noodle. It has to be a weeping willow." I turned to ask Lucy if she knew where one was, but she had already started running.

We found it down in the woods where the old pond used to be. A square of paper had been jammed between its branches. This time I grabbed the message first.

> *If in the summerhouse you'll peek,*
> *You might just find the prize you seek!*

We didn't have far to go. We had been led in a complete circle. I looked at Lucy. We were thinking the same thing again. Now that we were that close, I wasn't sure I wanted to find the surprise.

The summerhouse was dark. It was also empty. I was relieved in a way, but disappointed too. I felt kind of like the bride left waiting on the church steps, except it was the summerhouse steps. At the bottom of them was a ring of rocks marking the end of the trail.

Lucy scratched a chigger bite. "Well, somebody sure put one over on us!"

But Rob was staring at something in the summerhouse: something in the shadows. It moved!

"Hey, it's a box or something!" he yelled. He looked back at me and waited. "Ladies first," he said.

The box moved again. "Not on your life," I told him.

Lucy ventured as far as the steps. "Oh, come on! Whatever it is, it's in a box. It can't hurt us. Don't you even want to know what it is?"

My curiosity won out. I moved up to Lucy with my brother treading on my heels. "What if it's a snake?" he said. "What if it's a rattlesnake?"

"Oh, shut up," I told him. "It's probably just a joke or something. Besides, who's afraid of a little snake?"

I guess I shouldn't have said that, because just then the box turned over!

As soon as we finished screaming, Lucy and I worked up enough courage to take a second look. Rob had his face buried in my stomach. I pried him loose and squinted over the top of his head at the thing poking out of the box. A honey-colored ball of fur waddled out of its cardboard jail and fussed at us with little short yelps.

Lucy had a hcad start. She was holding the puppy on her lap before I could disconnect my brother from my waist.

The puppy seemed glad to see us. It told us so with its spongy red tongue and flashing banner of a tail. It bounced happily from Lucy to Rob to me and back again, doing crazy, crooked somersaults along the way. It was a funny-looking, ugly-cute dog with medium-long brown fur and dark velvet ears and tail. I made up my mind I was going to keep him.

"Who do you suppose left him here?" I asked Lucy as we sat on the summerhouse steps watching the puppy playing in the grass.

She shrugged and kept looking at the puppy. She didn't say anything.

"You know, don't you?" I shouted. "You knew the whole time!"

She giggled. I didn't think it was so funny. I didn't think it was funny at all, and I told Lucy so.

"I didn't know all of it—honest," she said. "I didn't know what was going to be in the box." She wasn't laughing anymore. "Please don't be mad, Peggy. I didn't do it to hurt your feelings. He told me it would be something good. And it is, isn't it? You do like it, don't you?"

"Sure I like it," I answered. "But whose is it?"

She grinned. "Yours, I guess. He said we could keep whatever we found, and I already have a dog."

Still, I wasn't convinced. "You keep talking about *he*. Who on earth is *he*?" I asked. "You won't turn to stone if you tell, will you?"

She looked at me for a minute. "No, but I promised. I gave my word."

Well, I couldn't argue with that, and I guess I never would have found out if something hadn't moved in the bushes just then.

CHAPTER 5

Come on out of there!" I shouted. "I see you."

It was a boy, slender with dark hair and a skinny kind of face. He was even taller than I was. He ambled out, grinning, and sat under the oak tree where the root bumps up. The first thing he wanted to know was how we liked the puppy.

"I really hated to give him up," he told us, "but my dog had three pups and Dad said we couldn't keep them. I didn't have any trouble giving away the other two, but this one . . . well, he's sort of scroungy-looking."

"Don't you talk that way about my dog!" I said. Then I added, "Well, I *hope* it's my dog."

The boy's name was Joel Henderson, he said, and he told us how he decided to lead us to the puppy. "I was watching when you moved in the other day, and I noticed that you didn't have a dog, so I talked Lucy into getting you into the woods so I could lay the trail. The rest was easy."

The puppy was crouching in the weeds, licking my sore toe. "Why didn't you just ask us if we wanted one?" I wanted to know.

He scratched the puppy's stomach a while before he answered. "I don't know. I just wanted to have some fun, I guess. There wasn't much else to do."

"Joel's new around here," Lucy laughed. "He hasn't gotten used to it yet."

Joel was still petting the puppy. I hoped he wasn't going to change his mind about giving it away. "Does your dad teach here at the college?" I asked.

"Yeah, in the history department. We only got here last month, and there's nobody on our street but a bunch of old maids! I'll be glad when school starts."

Rob shuddered. "Don't say that!"

"Well, it's better than doing nothing," Lucy agreed. "You'll be going to junior high, won't you, Joel?"

Joel stretched his long legs and watched the puppy waddle across the grass. "I'll be going into the eighth," he told us. He looked kind of lost. "Say, do you think you'll be able to keep the puppy?"

"I don't know," I said, "but I sure hope so. Rob has two hamsters, and my grandmother keeps a parakeet. I don't see why I can't have a pet too."

But it wasn't going to be that easy. We were eating watermelon on the back porch later that afternoon, trying to see who could spit seeds the farthest. So far, it was a tie between Joel and Rob. The puppy was napping under the hydrangea bush by the back steps when Danny came out to sweep the porch.

"My goodness alive! Where did that thing come from?" Her broom hung in midair.

Rob looked up hopefully. "We found it back there in the summerhouse."

"Isn't he cute?" I asked. "He looks a lot like a collie, don't you think?" (Danny loves Lassie!)

Danny leaned thoughtfully on her broom and stared at the puppy. "Looks more like a hound to me."

"Oh, I think it has some spaniel in it," Lucy offered. "You can tell by the ears."

"Well, let's just say it's an animal," Danny laughed, attacking the dust with her broom. "I expect it belongs to one of the neighbors."

Joel was looking guilty. "No, ma'am, it belongs to me, or

it did. I was kind of hoping Peggy and Robert could keep it."

Danny stopped sweeping. "Oh, I see," she said.

Rob reached over to stroke the dog's soft, fluffy neck. "He wants to stay here, Danny. Let us keep him, please?"

Danny only smiled in that "we'll see" kind of way that grown-ups have. "I think you'd better check with your mother about that," she said. "Now scat, all of you, before I sweep you off your feet!"

We found a shady spot in a clump of dogwoods in the front yard where our new pet thirstily lapped up a pan of milk that Rob had sneaked from the kitchen. I'm pretty sure Danny saw him do it, but she didn't say anything.

"What are you going to call him?" Lucy asked, as the puppy chased his empty pan around the grass.

I looked at our odd-looking mongrel. "Oh, I don't know. I can't think of anything clever. Besides, we might not get to keep him."

"Well, he still has to have a name," Rob reminded me. "We have to call it something. You can't just go around saying, 'Here Animal!'"

"Why not?" Lucy wiped a trickle of watermelon juice from her rumpled skirt. "I think it's a perfect name."

Joel grinned. "You know, I think you're right. I wish I'd thought of it myself. That's an animal if I ever saw one!"

"Okay," I said, "'Animal' it is." I rolled on my stomach to blot out the hot August sun. Animal pranced on my back with padded feet. It tickled! I guess we had eaten too much watermelon or something, because everyone was acting kind of quiet, like you do when you're sleepy and full. I had almost dozed off when the front gate clicked shut. It was like a gun-shot in the stillness. I looked up to see a tubby old man with a nose like a potato striding up the walk. And you wouldn't believe what he was wearing! He had on a big, white Panama hat and carried a cane. His spotless white shoes made important-sounding taps on the brick walk.

I poked Lucy. "Who's that?"

"Oh, it's just Judge Hardigree. He lives down the street."

She giggled. "Maybe he's coming to court your grandmother. He's an old bachelor, you know."

I looked the judge over. "He's not her type."

"Much too out-of-date," Joel whispered. "He belongs in an old movie; you know, where the guys carry canes and dance on tables and stuff."

Rob leaned against a tree and watched the judge bounce up the walk like a fat rubber ball. I guess he didn't want to miss it if the old guy happened to burst into song and dance.

Well, Judge Hardigree didn't exactly burst into song, but he came pretty close to popping the seam in his pants. It all happened so fast, it would be hard to say what caused him to fall. One minute his foot was on the bottom step leading to the porch, and the next it was in midair. And so was the judge!

Of course we all came racing out from our hiding place to see if he was hurt. It would be hard to ignore anybody as fat as the judge sprawled all over your front walk!

I don't think he was hurt, but he sure did seem surprised, and his round little face was as pink and wet as a wad of bubble gum. Joel and I helped him to his feet while Lucy dusted off his hat, which had fallen in the grass. It looked like somebody had stepped on it.

Judge Hardigree wheezed and groaned and jammed the hat on his blushing, fuzz-rimmed dome. I thought I heard somebody chuckle, but Lucy and Joel looked as worried as I was, and Rob was too scared to even come near us. It must have been my imagination.

Finally, after about a million stammered apologies from us and the judge too, we got him inside to a sturdy chair in the cool, dim parlor and let Danny take over from there. I wondered if he would ever be able to get up again.

I was really beginning to worry, because he didn't come out for a long, long time. And when he did, he left by the side door. I guess he wasn't taking any chances with our front steps again. I felt kind of sorry for him.

CHAPTER 6

After we had been here for a few days, Walnut Hill began to seem a little more like home. The story about our ancestor's lost invention made the old house seem more than just a drafty building in need of repairs. It became a mysterious manor with a secret all its own; and I love secrets.

Rob liked to talk about the great men of science who might have chatted in the tiny parlor or eaten in the huge dining room. But I concentrated on the ghost.

Did Walnut Hill really have a ghost? Sometimes at night, when everyone else was asleep, I would listen for the echo of an ancient footstep and watch for a flicker of ghostly light.

Danny showed me an old daguerreotype of our Great-Great-Great-Grandfather Summerville. He wore little square glasses and had a lot of wavy white hair. He was said to have been a small man, Danny told us, who wore a beaver hat and carried a gold-headed cane. He looked like a nice old fellow in the picture. I guess he would make a nice old ghost.

Somehow, though, I couldn't see that dignified old gentleman as a ghost.

Lucy didn't agree. We were sitting in the summerhouse working on the first edition of *The King's Creek Leader*.

"How about a story on the family ghost?" Lucy suggested.

"We haven't been introduced yet," I said. I don't even know

what kind of ghost it is."

"Danny said it's the ghost of the old inventor looking for his electric machine," Rob insisted. "That's the only ghost I know about."

"Maybe you could get an interview," Lucy said. "'A View from the Other Side by Great-Grandfather What's-His-Name!'"

"That's not funny." Joel was looking bored, but he sounded interested. "This is the first I've heard of an inventor. What did he invent?"

He quit looking so bored when I told him about the lost invention.

"Have you started looking for it yet?" he wanted to know.

"Well, we really haven't had much time," I admitted. "Besides, I don't even know where to start."

"Don't you have any idea where the old laboratory used to be?" Lucy asked.

"Hey, maybe it's in a dungeon!" Rob shouted. "That's where Doctor Frankenstein had his."

"Robert Patrick!" I yelled. "Don't you dare compare our Grandfather Summerville with Doctor Frankenstein!"

"Well, your house does have a basement," Lucy said in a matter-of-fact voice. "What's down there?"

I shrugged. "Mostly old boxes and stuff. We can look, though."

"Why don't we do that now?" Joel asked. "We don't have enough stuff for a newspaper yet."

"Danny won't mind," Rob added. "She's in a good mood today. She even invited Joel to supper."

I laughed. "I guess she's forgotten you gave us the puppy."

Thank goodness Mama's shop had had a successful opening the day the puppy came. We got to keep him without even an argument. To tell the truth, I think Mama liked him too.

Everybody seemed to be in favor of exploring the basement, so we made our way back to the house and plunged in—or down. The cellar was lighted by a single dim bulb that hung from the ceiling, so it was hard to see in the corners, but we turned up a lot of stuff: fruit jars with funny glass tops, an old baby carriage, and piles of dog-eared issues of the medical journal . . . but no invention. After we had been down there an hour or so, the smell of grilling hamburgers lured us outside again. Lucy was spending the night with me, and while she and I were making tossed salad, Joel helped Mama baste the meat with her special barbecue sauce. He was pretty good at flipping a burger.

After we got to know him better, Joel had told us that his parents were divorced. His mother lived in Europe somewhere with her second husband, and except for a maid who came now and then, he and his dad were pretty much on their own. They ate a lot of frozen stuff, Joel said, and it didn't seem to bother him. Except, I noticed, he never refused a home-cooked meal.

The food was great and I was starving—or at least I thought I was—but for some reason or other I felt kind of funny all during supper. I even let Rob have the last hamburger without so much as a scuffle.

"I heard you all were looking for the lost invention," Mama said, refilling Joel's glass with tea. "Did you find anything in the basement?"

"There's some good junk down there," Rob answered. "Can I have it?" Rob thinks all junk is good.

"There's not much there but spiderwebs," I said. "Ugh! They're everywhere."

"There couldn't be any invention down there," Joel added. "Not unless it has been sealed behind a wall somehow; and those walls look solid to me."

I quivered over my ice cream, and I don't think it was because of the dessert. "You mean like in Edgar Allen Poe's story, 'The Cask of Amontillado,' where this man gets sealed up alive? That gives me the creeps."

"Why would Great-Great-Great-Grandfather Summerville want to seal up his invention?" Rob asked.

"He wouldn't, I don't guess," Joel said. "Unless maybe somebody else did."

Danny was looking thoughtful. "I don't think you children are looking in the right place," she said. "Your Grandfather Summerville seemed to think the old lab was either above or below the library. Of course, the house has been searched again and again. I don't think it could be here."

"*Now* you tell us!" I groaned. "Well, where was the library?"

"I think it was one of the front rooms, probably the one on the left that we call the parlor. At least that's what your grandfather told me."

"Well, my room is over that," Mama laughed, "and I can assure you there's no invention in there!"

Rob grinned. "Have you looked in the closet?" he whispered.

"Finish your ice cream," Mama said.

We decided to give the basement another try, especially in that spot under the parlor. Joel poked in the corners with the big flashlight I used at camp. We found a rusty washboard, which Rob lugged up to his room, but that was all.

Lucy, Rob, and I were sitting on the back steps later that night, playing with the puppy. He was getting cuter every day. Joel hadn't been gone long when Animal started barking up a storm, so I thought he must be coming back for something. Soon we heard heavy footsteps on the front porch and peeped through the back hall to see a chubby silhouette in the doorway.

"Don't look now," Lucy whispered, "but I think the judge has come courtin' again."

"Oh, hush up!" I said. But sure enough, pretty soon we heard Danny joining him on the porch and the steady squeaking of their rockers as they chatted in the dark.

"What's he doing over here again?" Rob fussed. "He was here yesterday."

Danny and the judge kept the rocking chairs going for a long time after that. Lucy and I kept an eye on them from an upstairs window. It sure looked like Danny had a boyfriend. I don't know why I minded so much. I guess I knew our grandmother must want to be with folks her own age sometimes, but the judge? Why, he didn't seem like he'd be any fun at all.

I couldn't seem to get rid of that strange feeling I had had at supper. Even after Lucy and I finally went to bed, I couldn't get to sleep. After I had turned over for about the tenth time, Lucy sat up and threw back the covers.

"Do you always toss like this?" she complained. "If you don't go to sleep, I'm going home to my own bed where it's *quiet!*" She said the last word real loud.

I looked at the luminous dial on my watch. It was almost two o'clock. "I don't know what's wrong with me," I answered. "I'm sleepy, but I can't go to sleep. I keep getting little chills like a gust of wind is blowing on me."

Lucy felt my forehead. "Maybe you're sick. How do you feel?"

"I feel just fine," I told her, groping in the dark for my bedroom shoes. "I mean my head doesn't hurt; neither does my stomach. I just have a feeling something's going to happen."

Lucy cocked her head like a mother hen. "What you need is a good night's sleep."

"What I need is a midnight snack," I told her. "Come on and I'll fix us a Juliette Low Special."

Lucy didn't know what a Juliette Low Special was, of course. Most people don't even know who Juliette Low is unless they belonged to the Girl Scouts. She was the one who started Girl Scouting in this country. You see, I learned to make the Special at Girl Scout camp last summer. Everybody eats it there.

With a swish of the knife, I spread a piece of bread with peanut butter, added a frosting of sugar, and drizzled it with lemon juice. It was a masterpiece. Lucy watched grimly. "Ugh! I could never eat that!" she said.

I gobbled up the first piece and licked my fingers. . . .

Lucy licked her lips. "Just give me a little taste." She must have been starving. We finished off half a loaf of bread and washed it down with a pitcher of Kool-Aid. I was beginning to get sleepy, but Lucy was wide awake.

I almost jumped out of my skin when the kitchen door creaked open behind me and a cool draft hit me in the back where my pajamas didn't meet! But it was only Rob. For once I was glad to see him.

He looked relieved to see us too. "Gosh, I thought you were a ghost!" he whispered, rummaging in the refrigerator for a carrot. My brother eats more carrots than a rabbit. I wouldn't be surprised if he began to grow long ears. His nose is already turning a little pink at the end.

Lucy polished off the last of her bread and dabbed at her mouth with a napkin. Lucy is always neat, even at two-thirty in the morning. "Did we wake you up, or did you just get hungry too?" she asked.

Rob slid into an empty chair. "I heard something; I guess it was you. Anyway, here I am, and don't you two go off and leave me."

"We wouldn't think of it," I said. I was teasing, but I really meant it. Even *I* wouldn't want to be alone in that kitchen at night.

We finally persuaded Rob to bring his carrot up to bed. My eyes were beginning to droop as I stumbled up the steps. I heard a door close softly in the upstairs hall as we stepped onto the landing, and that woke me up a little. You might know either Mama or Danny would wake up and find us. I never get to have any secrets.

I was about to have one. The figure who waited for us in the hall was neither Mama nor Danny. I had never seen a ghost before, but I was seeing one now! I held to the smooth oak railing with a sweaty hand while drifts of cold air swirled around us. Could this really be happening to me? I closed my eyes. Maybe I *was* coming down with something.

When I opened my eyes, the figure was still there.

CHAPTER 7

I expected to see a vaporish little man in a beaver hat, but
our ghost was not a man; it was a woman, a young woman,
and somehow I wasn't afraid—just numb. Something kept
her from being pretty: her nose I guess. It was short and
turned up at the end, but her mouth was soft and sort of
wistful. She looked like she wanted to laugh and cry at the
same time. She had a friendly, pixie kind of face.

She waited for us at the top of the stairs with a half-smile
on her lips, and there was a sweet, musty smell about her
that lingered even after she had moved away from us. She
paused at a door at the end of the hall and looked back as if
she expected us to follow. The door led to the attic stairs.

Rob looked at me with a question in his eyes. He was still
clutching a half-eaten carrot. I nodded and the three of us
followed her down the hall in a curious, trancelike daze. The
quiet and the dark seemed to swallow us. The attic door was
half-open. I stumbled on the first step and groped for the
light switch. A dim yellow light flickered in the darkness and
we looked up to see the figure waiting in the shadows with
that same hopeful smile.

There was something sad about her: something in her
eyes. I looked at her face in the faint light of the attic bulb.
It was a gentle face. I think it would have been a happy face

if it hadn't been for those eyes. They were big and dark and kind of shimmering. I felt like I was looking right into her soul.

My mouth was dry and I had a funny feeling in my throat. Lucy moved up beside me. I grabbed her hand and it was wet.

"What do you want?" Lucy whispered. "Can you show us what you want?"

The woman seemed to glide to an old trunk by the window. I couldn't see her feet for the long folds of white skirt she wore, but it looked like they barely touched the floor. The dress was a lot like the ones you see in old family photographs, with the high lace neck and puffy leg-o'-mutton sleeves. She wore a wide blue sash and a tiny gold locket on a chain at her throat. She fingered the locket the whole time she stood there.

"She wants us to look in the trunk," Rob said. "There must be something in there she wants us to see."

There were a lot of old magazines piled on top of the trunk —more of Uncle Zeb's old medical journals, I guess. Anyway, they were heavy. The trunk wasn't locked, but the lid was so awkward it took two of us to lift it. The same sweet, musty scent drifted up around us. There were dresses inside, as well as a crumpled pair of slippers, a crushed straw bonnet, and some yellowed gloves. I didn't know what I was looking for. Suddenly my hand bumped against a bulky package at the bottom of the trunk. I drew out a large flat book, carefully wrapped in brown paper and tied with a string. "Is this what you wanted to show us?" I asked. We turned to the spot where she had been standing, but she was gone. We were alone in the attic.

I was shaking so, I could hardly open the door to my room. I don't even remember how I got there! I wrapped up in an old bathrobe and two blankets before I felt warm again. The three of us sat scrunched in the middle of my bed and carefully unwrapped the package. The paper was cracked and brittle, and the string fell apart in my hands. Lucy stroked the red leather cover and I noticed her hands were shaking; so were mine. It was a scrapbook. It said so in tarnished gold letters on the front. Inside was her name in spidery, old-fashioned handwriting: "Matilda Jane Summerville, Christmas, 1912." On the opposite page her faded photograph looked out with her hair in dark puffs around her face and a smile in her eyes. She was wearing the locket then too.

Lucy hadn't said much until then, and when I looked at her I knew why. She had been crying. She wiped her eyes with the back of her hand and sniffed loudly. I'm kind of embarrassed to cry in front of people, but not Lucy. When she felt like crying, she cried.

"What do you think happened to her?" she asked. "What can she want?"

I turned the yellowed page, and a crushed, dried rose fell into powdery pieces on the bed. "I guess she must need our help or she wouldn't be here," I said. "She looks like she's worried about something, real worried."

"Are you going to tell your mother?" Lucy picked up a small paper dance program by its creamy silken tassel. It had a picture of violets on the front; but it had been in the attic so long, the purple was flecked with brown spots. It made me feel empty inside.

I shook my head. "No, she trusts us or she wouldn't have come. Besides, they wouldn't believe us anyway. Can you imagine what Danny would say if I told her we'd seen a ghost?"

Lucy grinned. "She'd probably give us a dose of something awful and put us to bed."

Rob had fallen asleep in an uncomfortable-looking knot at the foot of my bed. I didn't have the heart to send him back to his room alone, so we made a pallet for him on the floor. He didn't even wake up when we rolled him onto it.

We wrapped the scrapbook back up in what was left of the brown paper and hid it on the top shelf of my closet in an empty puzzle box. Both of us were too sleepy to look through the scrapbook anymore that night. There was something special in that book that Aunt Matilda meant for us to find, and I wanted to be wide awake when we found it.

Danny jerked open the draperies the next morning at a little after nine, and the glaring sunlight slapped me smack in the face! I didn't know light could hurt that much. I heard her mutter as she stepped over the lump that was Rob, and our covers flew back with a snap. I could tell she was mad about something.

She came right to the point. "I want to know who did this."

I rubbed my eyes and blinked at her. She was holding a round, flat, and very dirty Panama hat. It looked like the judge's. The brim was ripped in two places, and the crown was as lopsided as the biscuits I tried to make last winter.

"Do you know where I found this?" Danny demanded.

Yawning, I shook my head.

"In the driveway after your mother left for work. It was right behind the tire!" She threw the squashed hat on my bed. "Just look at it! Are you going to tell me it got there by itself?"

I was too shocked and sleepy to talk. I'm not ready for the world when I get up in the morning, so I usually just pretend it's not there. It was hard to pretend Danny wasn't there.

Rob sat up in his blanket and stared at her with his mouth open. I don't guess we had ever seen Danny acting so funny. "We didn't do anything," he said finally. "Honest we didn't!"

Danny snatched up the hat and glared at us. "Well, it's a poor joke, whoever did it. A very poor joke!" She wasn't acting like our Danny at all.

CHAPTER 8

We're going to have to start doing our ghost-hunting in the daytime," I told Lucy that afternoon. "I can't take this midnight stuff."

Lucy laughed. "I guess ghosts get to sleep during the daytime, so it doesn't bother them to stay up late. By the way," she added, "did you hear anything more last night?"

I groaned. "I was so sleepy, she could have tap-danced on my bedpost, and I wouldn't have heard her."

Rob giggled. "That, I'd like to see!"

We had spent the morning at the pool—out of Danny's way. Joel was there, too, but he didn't speak to us. I guess he didn't want the other boys to know we were friends. Boys are weird!

Lucy and I had planned to tell him about Aunt Matilda's ghost, but we changed our minds when he acted like a snob. We could manage just as well without him!

Now, sitting in the summerhouse, we were searching through Aunt Matilda's scrapbook. So far we hadn't found much.

"Hey, look at this!" Lucy flipped to the back of the scrapbook. "It's a commencement program from some school."

I looked at the folded program. It looked a lot like the ones we use today:

Graduating Exercises
King's Creek Normal School
May 28, 1913

Lucy read it aloud.

"Wonder if they had an abnormal school!" Rob hooted.

"You belong in one," I told him. "That's just an old-fashioned name for a teachers' college."

He shrugged. "Strange name; I've never had a teacher who was normal."

We opened the folder. Rob was still snickering over his own joke. He was the only one who was.

"Look, there are only fourteen people in the whole class," Lucy said. "And all girls!"

"Teaching was about all a girl could do back then," I answered. "Poor things."

"Serves them right!" Rob hollered. "I believe in keeping women in their place."

I socked him.

Lucy was studying the fourteen names. "See anybody you know?" I asked.

"Nope. But I know some of these people must still be alive. One or two of them sound familiar, but I'm not sure."

I was reading over her shoulder. "Looks like everybody had a part in the program. It must have lasted all day. Here's Aunt Matilda: 'Piano Solo . . . "To a Wild Rose" . . . Matilda Jane Summerville.'"

"Well, we know she played the piano," Lucy said, "but that still doesn't get us anywhere. Let's see if there's anything more up front."

We thumbed through the yellowed pages and found a newspaper write-up about an ice cream party that Aunt Matilda had given on her "spacious front lawn." She must have invited everybody in town, and the article listed them all. There were more clippings about parties and picnics, and Aunt Matilda went to all of them. She seemed to have kept busy just having a good time. I was beginning to envy her a little bit. Then we found a notice of Aunt Matilda's being assigned to teach the fourth grade the coming fall in the King's Creek school system.

Lucy turned the pages carefully. (I let her hold the book because she had the cleanest hands.) "I still don't know what we're looking for," she said, "but I'm pretty sure we haven't found it yet."

But we were getting close. The next page turned up a handwritten invitation to a fraternity party from somebody named Calvin, and a fancy lace valentine from the same boy. It had gold cupids on it.

"Now we're getting somewhere!" I said.

Rob stared at the valentine and sniffed. "I think I'm gonna throw up!"

Lucy touched the red satin hearts and smiled. "I think it's pretty."

I thought it was, too, but I didn't say so, wondering what it would feel like to get a valentine like that.

Calvin turned out to be somebody special. A few minutes later we found his picture, still in its cardboard folder. He was slender and blond and he had nice eyes. He would have been kind of cute except for that mustache. If he were my boyfriend, I'd make him shave it off, but I don't guess it mattered to Aunt Matilda. Across the bottom of the photograph he had written, "Forever, Calvin." I wonder how long forever is.

We sat there and looked at the picture for a while and nobody said anything. I was afraid Lucy was going to cry again. Finally she said, "Poor Matilda! I wonder if they ever married?"

"I don't think so," I answered. "Danny said she died when she was young. I wonder what killed her?"

"I'll bet ol' Calvin did," my brother whispered. "Anybody who would send a valentine like that just has to be strange."

I gazed into the steady eyes of the photograph. "I don't think so," I said. "He doesn't look like a murderer."

Rob shrugged. "Jack the Ripper probably didn't either. Do you think there's anything about the lost invention in this book? I'm tired of all this sloppy valentine mush."

"What makes you think there's a connection between Great-Aunt Matilda and the lost invention?" I asked. "Great-Great-Great-Grandfather Summerville wasn't even alive when Aunt Matilda came along. He must have been an old man when he demonstrated the light in 1857, and she was only a young girl in 1912."

Rob looked worried. "Gosh, do you think we have two ghosts? Here we were, looking all over for the lost invention, when Aunt Matilda pops up!"

"I wish you wouldn't use that expression, *pops up*," Lucy said. "It sounds like Aunt Matilda jumps out of a toaster."

Our next discovery was an old letter from Calvin, mailed from a town in Alabama in September of 1913. The faded brown ink was a little hard to read, but we finally made it out.

"My Dear Matilda," he had written. "I have talked with Mr. Hutton here at the bank, and he says the position is mine if I want it. He and Father were great friends in college, and it seems that he thinks rather highly of the family, so I suppose he's willing to take a chance with me.

"If things work out here, we should be living happily in Alabama by this time next year. I know you will miss your family, but believe me, My Dear Matilda, you won't regret it!

"Look for me sometime next week. I miss you, Sweetheart." It was signed, "Your Calvin."

Rob had been reading over my shoulder. "Yuck!" he said, putting his had over his mouth. "Now I *know* I'm gonna be sick."

"Well, be sick somewhere else," I snapped. I turned to Lucy. "What do you think of that? Now we know they were planning to marry. I wonder why they didn't."

Rob giggled. "Calvin chickened out."

Lucy looked puzzled. "Maybe she got sick and died before they could marry. Let's see if there are anymore letters in here."

We searched every page, but no more letters turned up. I

guess Calvin wasn't much of a pen pal.

What did turn up was the very clue that Aunt Matilda had wanted us to find—only we didn't know that at first. It was a wedding invitation. At first I thought it might be Aunt Matilda's, but it turned out to be somebody I never heard of. We didn't even bother to read it. On that same page was a write-up of the wedding from the society page. "Miss Denton Weds Mr. Whiteside," the headline read. From there it went on to describe the ceremony down to the last detail. I stopped reading after the second paragraph.

"Why do you suppose she saved that?" I asked.

Rob said he didn't know and didn't care. I wondered if Aunt Matilda could turn him into a rabbit.

"Wait a minute!" Lucy gulped. "Maybe he married somebody else. What was that man's name again? The one on the invitation?"

"Whiteside, Richard Whiteside," I repeated.

Lucy grinned. "That's a relief. I was afraid, for a minute, our Calvin was a two-timer."

"Danny might know some of these people," I said. "She never actually lived here, but she used to visit a lot. She probably remembers some of them."

Lucy brushed the dirt from her shorts. "Then let's ask her. It's worth a try."

Rob had already started back to the house. "We can get something to eat while we're at it!" he yelled.

I heard a noise in the bushes behind us and turned to see Joel running to catch up. "Did somebody mention food?"

CHAPTER 9

Lucy and I gave Joel the silent treatment all the way back to the house, but I don't think he even noticed.

"What's in the scrapbook?" he asked in a half-interested voice.

"Oh, nothing." Lucy clutched the scrapbook a little closer.

"That's right!" my little brother chimed in. "A bunch of mush, mostly."

Joel gave the book a closer look. "It looks old. Where'd you find it?"

"You wouldn't believe us if we told you," I said. I could tell his curiosity was getting the better of him.

We found some apples in the refrigerator and took them out on the back porch, where Animal woke up from his afternoon nap and nuzzled under my arm. He was hungry, as usual.

"What's so secret about that scrapbook?" Joel asked, trying to act like he didn't really care.

Lucy looked at me and shrugged. "Oh, go on; tell him," she said.

I did. He lifted a cynical eyebrow and gnawed what was left of his apple. "Boy, do you have an imagination!" he snickered. "You really don't expect me to believe that, do you?"

That made me mad. "I don't care whether you do or not!

Come on, Lucy. Let's go find Danny and see if she can help."

Danny was on her hands and knees, weeding out the border by the front walk. She wasn't in much of a mood for looking through scrapbooks, but her curiosity won out when she saw the old photographs.

"Where did you find this old thing?" she wanted to know. "Whose was it?"

We told her whose it was and where we found it, but that's all we told her. Danny forgot all about her weeding and burrowed happily into the book. I had a feeling we were going to have trouble getting it away from her.

What interested her most was the picture of Aunt Matilda. "I didn't realize how pretty she was," she said. "She had a nose like your Uncle Zeb's. Your grandfather's was straighter."

Noses weren't my problem just then. "Danny," I began. "How did Great-Aunt Matilda die? Do you remember?"

"She stopped breathing, I guess." (Sometimes Danny can be as exasperating as her grandson!)

I tried to control myself. "Danny, I'm serious," I said calmly.

She worried her gardening glove away from the puppy and smiled. "Peggy, you forget that your grandfather was only a boy of ten when his sister died. I never met your Great-Aunt Matilda. John didn't remember too much about her." Danny gave me a funny look. "Why the sudden interest?"

"Oh, just curious." I tried not to look at Lucy.

Danny handed us back the book. "I always got the impression there was some kind of scandal," she admitted. "Your Uncle Zeb and Aunt Jane seldom spoke of her."

"What kind of scandal?" I asked.

"They never said, but there was a feeling that something wasn't quite right. Where there's smoke, there's fire, you know."

I said I knew, and poked the scrapbook under her nose again. "What about the people in here? Don't you remember any of them?"

Danny frowned at the list of names on the commencement program and shook her head. "One or two sound familiar, but I suppose they're dead and gone now."

"Hey, wait a minute! Don't forget the wedding invitation," Lucy reminded me.

Danny scanned the page in silence. She finally nodded, smiling. "Why, yes, I do remember Ida Whiteside. In fact, I think she still lives here."

I was so excited I must have been grinning all over! "Where does she live, Danny? Are you sure she's the one you know?"

Danny gave me one of her "grandmother" looks. "Well, an Ida Whiteside entertained for John and me when we were first married," she said. "And when your Uncle Zeb died, she brought a delicious marble cake. Unless there are two of them, I imagine she's the one."

Lucy slumped on the grass and stared at us with a peculiar expression. "Oh, you mean *that* Ida Whiteside? The one who lives in that big old house near the college? I know her."

"Well, why didn't you say so before?" I wanted to shake her.

"I don't know. It said Ida Denton on the invitation and we always just called her 'Miss Ida.' I guess I just wasn't thinking." Lucy wasn't looking very happy with our discovery.

"What's wrong with you?" I asked.

She ran a gentle finger down Animal's dark nose. "Miss Ida's kind of funny," she mumbled. "I'm scared of her."

Danny picked up her trowel and jabbed at some weeds. "I think she's become a little senile lately. They say she rarely goes out anymore."

"Do you think she'd mind if we came to see her?" I asked. "I mean, she wouldn't get mad at us or anything?"

Danny looked suspicious, but she didn't ask why. "Oh, I expect her bark is worse than her bite. Just telephone first and tell her who you are."

My hands were shaking so, I could hardly dial the number. In fact, the first time, I reached the bus station by mistake and had to start all over again. Lucy stood in the doorway as far away from the phone as she could get. I guess she figured old Miss Ida might jump through the telephone and grab her.

The voice that answered was old and frail. It wasn't much more than a whisper.

Now I was getting scared. "Mrs. Whiteside?" I asked. I hoped that I had dialed the wrong number again.

The voice came a little louder now. "This is Minnie Bell," she croaked. "Miss Ida's resting now. Who's calling, please?"

I told her my name and who I was, and that we wanted to talk with Miss Ida. She didn't say anything for a while after that. In fact, I was beginning to wonder if she had hung up on me. I guess she wasn't used to getting phone calls from a bunch of nosy kids.

"My grandmother said that Miss Ida has been around a long time," I began. (No, that didn't sound right!) "I mean, I heard she was one of King's Creek's older citizens," I added. "What I'd really like is an interview for our neighborhood paper, *The King's Creek Leader.*" I was glad she couldn't see my red face.

Silence again. "The what?"

"*The Leader*, my newspaper," I repeated. "I want to write a story about Miss Ida. Do you think she could see me for just a little while?"

Lucy was making frantic signals to get me to hang up. She looked like she might explode any minute.

"Who did you say this is?" the woman asked again.

I gave her a brief rundown on my family history.

She sighed. "Just a minute." She must have dropped the phone then, because it sounded like a gun went off in my ear. When she picked up the receiver, her voice seemed stronger. "Miss Ida said she would be glad for you to drop by tomorrow," she told me. "I'm sorry we can't ask you over today, but she didn't sleep well last night. I'm afraid she's a little tired."

I grinned at Lucy, "Oh, that's okay," I answered happily. "Tomorrow's fine. See you then!" I waited until I had hung up to give my victory yell.

Lucy looked paler than usual. "Why on earth did you tell her that?" she shouted.

"Tell her what?"

"That stuff about an interview!" she squealed. "You're not really going through with it, are you?"

"Not me—us! And why not? It's the best way I know to get her to see us. Besides, people like to be recognized. I'll bet she makes a good story, too."

Lucy shuddered. "Well, you can go by yourself. She gives me the creeps. Once, when I was in the first grade, my sister promised me a quarter if I would put a dead bird on her front steps. I was just dumb enough to do it, and her housekeeper ran me out of the yard with a broom!"

I laughed. "Do you blame her? Who wants a dead bird on her steps?"

"That's not all, either," Lucy said. "Her husband was killed a long time ago in the First World War, and they say she keeps his ashes on the mantel in a big urn!"

"Don't be such a super-silly! You know we have to go there. Miss Ida is the only link we have to Aunt Matilda's secret."

Lucy thought about what I said. Finally she took a deep breath as if she were about to jump into a cold pool for the first time. "Well, okay," she agreed. "But if we see anything that even slightly resembles an urn, I'm leaving!"

CHAPTER 10

The time had come for us to look for Aunt Matilda's grave,
I told Lucy later that day. We had been putting it off and we
knew it. It's one thing to be visited by somebody's spirit, and
another to actually look at the grave. I really didn't want to
see it, but I knew we had to.

When Danny came in from her gardening, I asked her
where Aunt Matilda was buried.

"Why, Peggy Patrick!" she said. "You're getting downright
morbid. What's all this fascination with dead people and
cemeteries?" She sniffed at a pot of fresh pole beans sim-
mering on the stove and gave them a poke with a spoon. I
remembered I was hungry.

"What's wrong with being interested in history?" I argued.
"You're the one who told me I should remember all the people
who lived here before me."

Danny bit her lip. I could tell I had her there. "She's in
the family plot at Saint Luke's churchyard, I think. Somewhere over in the corner near that big magnolia . . . but you
can't go now. I'm going to need a little help in the kitchen. It's
almost six o'clock."

"Golly, I didn't know it was that late!" Lucy gulped.
"Mother will be looking for me, too. My sister, Evelyn, left for
camp this week, and now I have to do twice the work!"

Danny was slicing lemons for the tea. "You poor, poor dear," she said, grinning. "You must be exhausted."

Lucy gave her a funny look. Sometimes she can't tell when Danny's teasing.

Rob invited Joel to stay for supper, of course. He took one sniff of the beans and accepted. We had cold ham, too, and some homegrown tomatoes the judge had brought by. I wasn't going to eat them, but I did.

After supper Rob took Joel up to his room to show him his latest invention. Joel should have felt honored. Rob never even lets me peek at his junk. I heard them whispering in there when I went upstairs to get my flashlight. Lucy and I were planning to explore the old cemetery, and I didn't want to get caught out there in the dark.

As I started back downstairs, the door to Rob's room opened. He poked his head over the stair railing and yelled for me to wait.

I tried to hide the flashlight under my T-shirt. "Lucy and I have our own plans," I said.

"I know where you're going," Rob told me, "and I have just as much right to go as you do!"

Well, I couldn't argue with him there. I suppose he did; but if Joel wanted to go, he'd better keep his smart remarks to himself. I told him so.

"I'm just curious," Joel admitted. "I can't believe you three think you've really seen a—"

"Shhh!" I warned him. "Whether you believe it or not, don't say anything to anybody, please!"

Joel nodded, looking puzzled. I guess he thought he had gotten mixed up with a real bunch of weirdos.

We wandered over to Lucy's house. The sun was still bright and I felt silly carrying a flashlight. Animal trailed along behind us, bubbling over with happiness at being allowed past the front gate. He poked his little black nose into everything, and sometimes things poked back.

Lucy had just finished stacking the dishwasher when we came by. She was supposed to sweep the kitchen, but her mother let her out of it. Lucy says sometimes she leaves crumbs on purpose so her mother will stop asking her.

Saint Luke's is over on the other side of the college, and the old cemetery is behind it. We had to pass Miss Ida's house to get there. Old and dark, it looked lost and sad behind a yard jammed with overgrown shrubbery and shaggy trees. There was an old stone wall around it, built of gray, moss-streaked rocks.

Nobody spoke as we walked by, but I grinned at Lucy as we glanced behind us. "You must have been out of your mind to put a dead bird on her steps," I said. "I wouldn't do it for a dollar."

"Neither would I now," she admitted. "But then I didn't have any better sense."

There was a gray wall around the cemetery, too. There must have been a rock quarry nearby. A lot of the college buildings were built of the same stuff. I hoped they had run out. It was depressing.

Our family lot was near the front somewhere. I thought it was going to be easy to find because it had a black iron fence around it, but so did everyone else's. We finally found it, though, and they were all there: from Great-Great-Great-Grandfather Summerville on down. My daddy isn't buried there as he's not really a Summerville; he just married one. But my grandfather is, and over in a corner beyond his grave was Aunt Matilda's.

It was marked by a simple slab with her name and the dates of her birth and death; that was all. She was only twenty when she died. A granite marker sure doesn't tell much about twenty years of living. I guess if you leave enough love behind, it doesn't matter.

We scattered all over the lot looking for Calvin's grave, but he wasn't buried with Summervilles. We had studied every stone. Maybe he wasn't even dead yet, I thought; but somehow I knew he was.

We sat on the cool rock wall in that misty in-betweenness that comes just before dark in the summer. I was feeling sort of discouraged, but then graveyards aren't exactly cheerful places.

Rob was studying the dates on Aunt Matilda's weather-beaten headstone. "Hey, I just thought of something," he began. "We could check with the newspaper here for old copies of the paper near the time she died. We might find out something."

Sometimes my brother comes up with a fairly intelligent notion. "You're right," I said. "Most papers keep old records on file, don't they?"

Joel shook his head. "Not small weeklies, or at least not that far back."

"Well, they might," Lucy argued. "It's worth a try."

I squinted at the grimy black carving on the granite. "She died in January: January 18, 1914. Does that date sound familiar?"

Rob shrugged. "Why should it? None of us were around in 1914."

"Well, there could have been a train wreck or an epidemic or something," I said. "Maybe Miss Ida can tell us something tomorrow. I hope she remembers."

Joel stretched. It was getting kind of late and we really hadn't found out anything. "We don't even know this Calvin's last name," he said. "I'm not about to hunt all over the cemetery, reading every stone. Besides, it's getting almost too dark to see."

Lucy nudged me and grinned. "Joel wants to go home. He hasn't had anything to eat in almost two hours."

"Come to think of it," Rob added, "I could use a couple of carrots, myself."

Still I sat on the wall. The rock was cold and hard beneath my bare legs and I was too lazy to move. Rob was whistling "Jeremiah Was a Bullfrog" under his breath. It was his favorite song. Animal had chased a squirrel around the trunk of a big oak tree in the next lot and was falling all over the knotty roots, barking like crazy.

Then I felt the cold again: not only in my legs, but clean

through to the tips of my fingers. It felt like I had swallowed a snowball in one gulp.

Rob stopped whistling and backed into the wall next to Joel. The dog gave a low whimper and crawled under a low bush with his tail between his legs.

That same smell surrounded us—like long-pressed carnations—and I knew Aunt Matilda had come.

CHAPTER 11

Beginning with a light, like a dim bulb with a veil over it, it slowly took form: wispy at first, with a dull kind of glow. It moved. Aunt Matilda was looking back at us again, urging us to follow her with her great, sad eyes.

Lucy's long fingernails were cutting into my wrist. She broke the skin in three places!

Joel was just sitting there, half on the wall and half off, with his long legs stretched out and his mouth hanging open. I wouldn't have traded that moment for a million dollars.

Aunt Matilda drifted slowly across the graveyard, in and out among the slanted markers in her billowy, white dress. It was getting hard to keep up with her. Finally she came to the end of the very last lot where the rambling, gray wall rose shoulder high to shut out the rest of the world. I wondered if she would walk through it.

She didn't. She only reached a filmy arm across and looked over the top at something on the other side. Her eyes were asking—no, begging—for help.

I had seen that same look once in the eyes of a stray dog that had been hit by a car. It was a lost, hurt look. A kind lady had come and taken the dog to the vet; at least the dog had found somebody who cared enough to help. And I knew that was what Aunt Matilda needed from us.

The woods had closed in on the lonely grave on the other side of the wall. I knew whose it was before we looked. There was a rusty, spiked fence around it, all grown over with dust-covered vines. Except for the weeds, the ground around it was bare. There were trees behind us: oaks, pines, dogwood, sweet gum. Trees, weeds, and silence.

We scrambled over the wall. Joel went first and gave the rest of us a hand. I could easily have jumped it myself, but this was no time to argue for women's liberation.

"Watch where you step," I whispered to Rob. "There might be a snake in there." But the only thing that moved was a surprised cricket. We were probably his only visitors in ages.

Joel jerked a handful of yellowed grass away from the stone so we could read the inscription. I shone my flashlight on the letters.

CALVIN A. HARDIGREE

BELOVED SON OF

HENRY AND MARY ANN HARDIGREE

b. May 3, 1892

d. Sept. 23, 1913

Lucy looked at me, then at the stone, and back to me again. "Well," she said finally. "What do you think of that?"

From the other side of the dark wall I thought I heard a sob: a faint, low whisper of a sob. Then she was gone.

We didn't waste any time getting home. The lighted windows of Walnut Hill looked warm and friendly. I was glad to be home again, ghost or no ghost.

We left Animal on the back porch and tried to slip in without being seen. No such luck! Mama was sitting at the kitchen table, shelling field peas into a big brown bowl.

Danny was stirring a pan of boiled custard so she would have some to send over to Miss Ida the next day. Danny's always sending boiled custard to somebody. If I were Miss

Ida, I'd rather have a big, fat chocolate cake.

Mama looked up from her field peas. "Did you find what you were looking for?"

I grinned at Joel. He was still pale. "We sure did," I said.

We escaped into the playroom and shut the door. The playroom is where Uncle Zeb used to have his office, but we had the partitions removed. Now it's a long, narrow room with a lot of windows.

Joel sank into Danny's old armchair and draped his stringy legs over the side. "I think I know what the problem is," he said. "For some reason or other, this Calvin was buried outside the churchyard. She wants him with her; it's as simple as that."

I tried to sneer, but I'm not very good at sneering. "Oh, have you finally become a believer?"

"If I could explain it any other way, I would," he said. "I never thought I'd admit it, but—yes, we've seen a ghost!"

Lucy leaned against the window seat and frowned. "But what can we do about it? Why was he buried out there in the first place?"

"That's what I hope we'll find out from Miss Ida tomorrow," I told her.

She made a face. "I was hoping you'd forget."

"Oh, come on, Lucy," I said. "If you're not afraid of a ghost, surely you can face up to one little old lady!"

Rob was looking worried. "The next time we see Aunt Matilda, remind me to ask her something."

"Ask her something!" I snorted. "What in the world would you ask her?"

"About Great-Great-Great-Grandfather Summerville's invention. She might know where it is."

"What makes you think she knows that?"

"Well, they're both ghosts, aren't they? They probably buddy around together."

"You really mean it, don't you?" I laughed. "I doubt if she could answer you even if you did ask her. She never actually talks, you know."

"Huh!" he grunted. "If we can help her, she can very well give us a hand too."

"Rob," I said, "she's gonna turn you into a rabbit yet!"

CHAPTER 12

Danny made me put on a dress the next morning just to visit Miss Ida. When Lucy showed up in shorts, she made her go home and put on a dress, too. Of course Lucy didn't mind so much, but I suffered enough for both of us. Danny said that Miss Ida probably wasn't used to little girls running around with no clothes on. I argued that she couldn't be so old she had never seen a pair of shorts, but it didn't do me any good. When my grandmother makes up her mind, she can be as stubborn as any mule—and stubborner than most.

At last we passed inspection and started off down the street with the boiled custard sloshing around in a plastic refrigerator jar. I had even brought along a pencil and pad to make me look official, although I don't remember seeing any other reporters taking boiled custard along on their assignments.

Lucy started out in one of her giggling moods, but the closer we got to Miss Ida's house, the quieter she became. When we finally got there and pushed open that squeaky front gate, I practically had to drag her down the walk.

The woman who came to the door must have been Minnie Bell, I guessed. Miss Ida's housekeeper was short and fat, and was probably close to eighty herself, but her hair was as shiny and dark as my black patent leather boots. (A smudge of dye still showed on her forehead.) Lucy breathed a sigh of relief as we followed Minnie Bell down the long, gloomy hallway. I guess she had forgotten about the dead bird incident. The fat housekeeper moved slowly, using a cane. Her tiny gold earrings bobbed with every step. Finally she showed us to a door near the back of the house and hobbled off to the kitchen with the custard.

The door was open a crack, but I figured we'd better knock anyway, just to be sure. A small voice told us to come in. We nearly didn't see her at first because she was so tiny, but then I realized someone was standing behind the big chair by the window.

"The marigolds aren't doing well this summer," she said happily. Two bright blue eyes peered over the chair. "But then I never really cared for marigolds, anyway . . . Minnie Bell will put them in."

She must not have been much over five feet tall, but she was as straight as a toy soldier. She was even what Danny would call frail, yet I'll bet she could hold her own with anybody. She took firm steps to greet us as Lucy and I waited in the doorway. No walking cane for her! As she came closer, I saw that she was pretty, like a storybook grandmother, and her face had hardly any wrinkles at all. She stooped over Lucy and gave her an almost-kiss. "You must be Zeb's niece; or is it grandniece? You have the Summerville smile."

I wondered whose smile she thought *I* had. Lucy giggled. "Oh, this is Peggy. My name is Lucy Parrish."

"Parrish? Parrish?" Miss Ida mumbled. "Why, you must be the hardware Parrish. We buy all our seeds there, you know."

Lucy was sending me signals again. Her daddy was in the insurance business. (She told me later that her grandfather had run a hardware store, but that he had been dead for at least five years.)

Miss Ida led us to a group of chairs by the window, where there was a small table with a potted fern, some worn-looking books, and an old sewing basket. I could tell that she sat there a lot and I didn't blame her. There were all kinds of roses in the garden under her window. It hadn't been weeded in years, but it was still pretty in a wild sort of way. I thought of the garden in "Sleeping Beauty" after one hundred years had passed. This one looked about halfway there.

"I hear I'm to be interviewed for some sort of newspaper," Miss Ida began as we sat down. "Would you girls like some lemonade first?"

Lucy shook her head politely, and I was too excited to be thirsty.

I soon found out I had come to the right place to get a story on the history of King's Creek. To hear Miss Ida tell it, she had been there since the beginning. I felt a little like I was talking with Eve in the garden of Eden.

I asked her if she ever heard anything about Great-Great-Great-Grandfather Summerville's invention. She had, of course, but she didn't know what happened to it either.

"My grandmother thinks the old lab was near where the library used to be," I told her. "But we've practically combed the basement, and there's no invention there."

Miss Ida pulled a dead leaf from her fern and stared out at the rose garden. "You know, they might have meant the campus library," she said finally. She looked interested. "When I was a girl, I believe it was in an old frame building near the Main Hall. I wonder, now: did that old thing burn down?"

"Say, that's a great idea," I said. "I never even thought of that." I waited, hoping she would tell me more. She did, but not about the lost invention. She was off on another subject, and then another. I wrote it all down—or most of it. There was a story there somewhere, and a good one, too.

"You certainly don't look like the Summervilles," Miss Ida told me. She was examining me with those probing blue eyes. "But then, your grandfather—John—he didn't either with that head full of red hair. I believe you have a dash of it too."

"Did you know him very well?" I asked. "He died before I was born, so I never knew him at all."

Miss Ida smoothed an imaginary wrinkle from her skirt.

"He was just a boy when I married, and quite a bit younger than I was." She smiled. "He used to give your Aunt Matilda and me some trying times, but I suppose most little brothers do that."

Lucy leaned forward in her chair. "Can you tell us about Peggy's Aunt Matilda, Miss Ida? We found an old scrapbook of hers in the attic, and it had your wedding invitation in it. You must have been good friends."

Miss Ida laughed. "I should say we were! We had some good times together, Matilda and I. She was in my wedding, you know; and I would have been in hers, too, if she had ever married." Her voice dropped to a whisper. "Matilda was a pretty girl and she wasn't afraid to have fun. She was the kind of person who enjoyed life, but life wasn't kind to Matilda. It cheated her in the end."

Miss Ida's words were bitter. I wondered what she meant.

My voice shook. "I know she was planning to marry," I said, "but we found her fiancé's grave; he died before they could go through with it. Then in a few months, she died too. What happened, Miss Ida? Was there some kind of epidemic?"

Miss Ida said a strange thing. "An epidemic of shame!" she snapped. "Calvin was a good boy, and they blamed him for things he didn't do, even accused him of taking his own life. I never believed a word of it!"

Lucy gasped. "You mean he was supposed to have committed *suicide?*"

"Why do you think he's buried outside the churchyard?" Miss Ida asked calmly. "Your aunt and I were very close, and Calvin was in love with her . . . I know he was. They were planning a future together, and they were both so happy. Why would a man like that risk everything by committing a crime?" Miss Ida stood up and brought her small hand down with a thud on the back of the upholstered chair. "Calvin would never have taken his own life—never!"

I forgot about my pad and pencil and went to stand beside her. "What crime do you mean?" I asked. "What did they think he did?"

Lucy had forgotten she was nervous. "Did Peggy's Aunt Matilda kill herself over Calvin, or did she just die of grief? What happened to her, Miss Ida?"

"People don't die of grief, Lucy," Miss Ida said. "Not even back then; but it doesn't make them any healthier, either. I guess, in a way, Matilda did want to die. If she had been stronger, she might even be here today. But it wasn't really sorrow that killed her. Scarlet fever did that."

Lucy was looking kind of funny. "Why, I had scarlet fever just last year," she said. "I had a bad throat and a rash, but that was all. I don't think I even missed a week of school."

"That was because you had penicillin," Miss Ida told her. "Doctors didn't know about that when Matilda was sick. Of course, not everyone who had the fever died, but many did."

We watched as she crossed the room and opened the drawer of an old desk in the corner. "I expect our friend Minnie Bell will be here in a minute to run you off," she said over her shoulder. "If we hurry through the back way here, I might just have time to cut a few of my roses for you before she finds us." Finally she found the scissors she was looking for and closed the drawer with a bang. "You would like some roses to take home to your mothers, wouldn't you?"

"Oh, yes," I answered as we followed her into a small back room. "Are you sure it won't be too much trouble?"

Miss Ida laughed. "It does me good to give Minnie Bell the slip now and then. Besides," she added, "I know you'll want to hear the story about poor Calvin, and perhaps you'd better. I can see Matilda has been to see you, too. I hope she has finally found someone who can help."

CHAPTER 13

Several seconds went by before what she had said sank in. Sometimes I'm kind of slow. "Do you mean that Aunt Matilda has been to see you, too?"

Miss Ida nodded. "Only twice, and never here; I don't think she can come here." She stepped over to the mantel and carefully lifted a heavy china urn. Globs of pink and white roses were painted on the front, and the handles gleamed with a dull gold.

Lucy was looking sick. I was feeling sick.

"Have a peppermint," Miss Ida offered, poking the gruesome urn under our noses. "I have to hide them in here from Minnie Bell. She tells me they're bad for my health." Miss Ida popped a red-and-white-striped candy into her mouth and smiled.

Lucy and I took one, too. For once I was glad I had so many freckles. Maybe Miss Ida wouldn't be able to see I was blushing.

We stepped down into the garden, closing the door softly behind us. There were stone benches around a sundial: they looked like they had been there forever. We sat there, hidden from the house by a tangle of overgrown roses.

"Matilda came to me twice," Miss Ida told us. "The first time was just before your Uncle Zeb died. Jane had passed away a few years before, I believe, but Thomas was there at home. I took some soup over to Walnut Hill. Zeb always loved my vegetable soup. As I was leaving, I saw Matilda. There was no doubt about it! It was Matilda, as plain as day. She was standing on the landing of the stairs, looking down at me."

"What did you do?" I asked. "Did she say anything?"

"No, she didn't have to. She just stood there and looked at me as if to say, 'Ida, why don't you do something? Why don't you help me?' I knew what she wanted, but I couldn't help." Miss Ida's eyes were wet as she looked at me. "What could I do?" she asked sadly.

Lucy answered and I was glad. I had that terrible knot in my throat again. "We know just how you feel," she said. "Did you say you saw her again after that?"

Miss Ida thought for a minute. "It was sometime last June, I think, because I had gone over to the cemetery to put some hydrangeas on Richard's grave. Richard is my husband," she explained, "gone these many years."

I thought for a horrible minute that she had forgotten we were there. She smiled and stared at the roses as if she expected to see him there. "How he loved flowers," she said. "Roses, especially, He planted many of these."

"You saw her in the cemetery?" asked Lucy, trying to remind her politely.

Miss Ida nodded. Aunt Matilda had appeared to her in the graveyard, just as she had to us, to remind her that Calvin was still buried outside the churchyard.

I frowned. "Well, why did they put him out there? Do they always do that with suicides?"

"They did then," Miss Ida answered. "Of course his family wanted him in their own plot, but some of the parishioners objected. The churchyard is consecrated ground, you see."

"But couldn't some of his family have him moved now?" Lucy wanted to know. "Wasn't he related to the judge?"

Miss Ida smiled. "Yes, but that was then and this is now. I really don't think they care; and then, too, why stir up old scandals? The Hardigrees are better off forgetting Calvin!"

"That's awful!" I sputtered. "It's just not fair! The next time that fat old judge comes to see Danny, I'll just ask him why they haven't done something about it."

Lucy groaned. "And a fat lot of good that'll do you! The judge is running for office, didn't you know?"

"What?"

"That's right: state senator. So you see, this isn't the best time to dig up the family skeleton."

I shivered. "Lucy! That's not funny."

"She's right, though," agreed Miss Ida. "Judge Hardigree isn't going to advertise the fact that his Uncle Calvin was accused of embezzling funds from the local bank. I don't care how long it has been."

"Is that what Calvin did?" shouted Lucy.

Miss Ida tugged at a honeysuckle vine which was choking her red climbing rose. "That's what they *said* he did," she reminded her. "And it's true, the money was missing. But I can't believe Calvin took it. He didn't have any reason to take it; and besides, he wasn't the sort."

I dodged a suspicious bee who must have felt I was after his treasure. The garden was filled with their humming, but Miss Ida didn't seem to mind. She was snipping away at roses of all colors and sizes, enough to fill a bunch of vases.

I sniffed at a yellowish-pink bud. It was a Peace rose, Miss Ida said. "Why did they think it was Calvin who embezzled the money?" I asked her.

"The bank was the Hardigree family business, you see. Calvin's father was the first president. His two sons, Arthur and Calvin, joined him in the family business, but I don't think they got along so well together. There was no love lost between them. The judge, now, is Arthur's son."

"Maybe Arthur took the money," I said.

"Didn't they ever find it?" Lucy wanted to know.

I was sorting the roses into colors: pink, red, yellow. "Find what?"

"The money, of course. The money that was embezzled from the bank."

Miss Ida sat down on the bench beside us. "I don't think they did. Of course the Hardigrees hushed the whole thing up. To hear them tell it, the money was never missing. But you can't cover up for a dead man, and Calvin was definitely dead! There had to be a reason for it."

Miss Ida looked very small sitting there in the garden, and suddenly she looked very old, too. She shrugged. "The whole town knew about the money, but old Mr. Hardigree put back whatever was missing so there wouldn't be an investigation."

"What do you think, Miss Ida?" I asked. "Do you think Calvin took the money?"

"Of course I don't. But the evidence—or what there was of it—pointed to him. Arthur was the oldest, and I think he wanted to run things." Miss Ida closed her eyes against the sun. I guess she was remembering. "Just before all this happened," she went on, "Calvin left town for a few days. He had been back only a day or so when they found his body in the old rock quarry at the foot of a cliff. Then, of course, they noticed the money was missing . . . convenient, wasn't it? Folks began to talk about how Calvin had seemed worried about something." Miss Ida frowned. "Sometimes I think people like to assume the worst. They certainly did in Calvin's case."

Lucy's eyes were shiny wet. "Poor Matilda! It must have been awful for her."

"It nearly killed Matilda," Miss Ida answered. "She continued teaching, but she was like someone in a daze. The life had just drained out of her. When the fever came, I think she just gave in to it."

"Miss Ida!" Minnie Bell squeezed through the porch door and pounded her cane on the tile floor. "You ought not be out here in this hot sun. Come on inside, ya hear?"

Miss Ida looked at me and smiled. "I'm coming, Minnie. Be there in a minute." The door squeaked shut.

Lucy and I thought of Calvin's letter at the same time. We took turns telling Miss Ida about it.

"It was written from somewhere in Alabama," I said, "and

from what he said in the letter, I think he was planning to leave King's Creek."

"Could be because of his brother," muttered Lucy. "Since they didn't get along and all, maybe Calvin just wanted to start over in a new place."

Miss Ida nodded. "You know, I think I do remember something about his getting a job in Alabama. Matilda was afraid to tell her parents they wouldn't be living here."

"Why not?" Lucy asked. "They were grown, weren't they?"

Miss Ida laughed. "Well, times were a little different then. Back in those days, parents never considered their daughters grown." She rose to go. "I'll get some newspapers for those roses. The thorns can be painful."

She glanced at her shabby garden and shook her head. "It makes me sad to see it this way—it really does. But I'm not as strong as I used to be, and of course it's out of the question for Minnie Bell." She looked at Lucy and me. "It's almost impossible to get any outside help for the little I can afford to pay. I don't suppose you would know of anyone, would you?"

I thought for a minute. "I would offer to help myself," I said, "but I probably wouldn't know a flower from a weed; and my brother's too young."

Lucy grinned. "Hey, how about Joel? He doesn't have much to do. I think he'd kinda like it."

"I do hope so," admitted Miss Ida. "It would be a treat just to see the garden walks clear again."

She wrapped the roses in some old newspapers from a stack on the porch and followed us to a rusty garden gate.

Minnie Bell's screeching voice came again, searching us out. "Miss Ida? You still out here? It's almost dinnertime!"

"Oh, for goodness' sake!" Miss Ida snapped. "Can't I have a minute's peace? I'm coming, Minnie, I'm coming!" Behind a giant boxwood, she made a funny face and smiled at Lucy and me. "Treats me like an infant!" she fussed.

Just before she went inside, she put her tiny hand on my arm. She was stronger than she looked. "Do something for

Matilda if you can," she said. "There's not much I can do; I'm getting old now and tend to be absentminded and forgetful. . . . I suppose some people think I'm foolish. It wouldn't help Matilda by having an addled old woman going around babbling about seeing ghosts."

The gate clanged shut behind us. "We will!" I promised. *I hope*, I added silently to myself.

CHAPTER 14

I didn't get a chance to tell Rob all the good stuff about my visit with Miss Ida when I got home. Lunch was on the table and Danny was there, so I had to watch what I said. I think he was surprised to even see me come back alive after what Lucy had said about the urn.

Danny acted almost surprised about my interview with Miss Ida. I don't think she expected it to turn out so well. I guess she knows now that I'm a genuine, honest-to-goodness reporter, in spite of the boiled custard! Anyway, I told her all about Miss Ida and her bossy housekeeper, Minnie Bell. Danny laughed and said she thought Minnie Bell was the one who needed the housekeeper. That was when she decided we ought to ask Miss Ida and the judge over to dinner. "It's time we did a little entertaining around here," she told us, filling my bowl a second time with homemade vegetable soup. "After all, they're both old family friends."

I looked at Rob and grinned. I thought it was a terrific idea, I said. The judge and Miss Ida. . . . Aunt Matilda would be sure to drop in that night.

After lunch Rob wanted to work on some secret weapon or other out in the shed, but I dragged him over to the campus to see if the old frame library Miss Ida had mentioned was still there. We found the Main Hall without any trouble.

It was big and gray and ugly like most of the old buildings in King's Creek, and it looked like it would be around for another hundred years, growing even older and uglier.

The library next to it wasn't made of stone. It wasn't wooden either, or even old. It was brick and modern in a funny abstract design with a lot of glass and a flyaway roof. It was a sure bet the long-lost invention wasn't in there.

We meandered around in the Main Hall a while, looking for somebody who could tell us what had happened to the frame library. The registrar's office was open, but he turned out to be a young man who had been there only a few years. He sent us to see Professor Pittman in the English department. "He'll know if anyone will," he laughed, and when we found the professor, we knew what he meant.

Professor Pittman might not have been as old as the buildings, but he was the same color: suit, hair, beard . . . everything about him was gray. If he had worn a robe and carried a scythe, he would have looked like Father Time in all the New Year's cartoons. Professor Pittman was a professor emeritus, which means he's retired but still has the title. Joel told us later that Professor Pittman was a poet—and a pretty good one, too.

He didn't seem especially glad to see us when we knocked on his office door. He looked up from a pile of a dozen open books and peered at us over the rim of his glasses. But when he heard we were interested in the history of the college, he invited us in and even offered us some candy from a red-and-white-striped sack. It was licorice, though, so we didn't take any.

The professor's voice matched his hair—soft and wispy, like faraway clouds trailing across the sky. Sometimes we could hardly hear him. And he talked kind of funny, too. His *R*'s sounded like *H*'s sometimes, and his *A*'s like *E*'s. That was because his people had come from the low country of South Carolina, Danny said later. Rob thought it was funny when the professor said "leh-dy" for *lady*, but I liked to hear it—even if I couldn't understand it all.

The old frame library had burned in 1925, the professor said. It was replaced by the ivy-covered brick building across from Main Hall, only now that's being used by the art department. The college outgrew the brick library several years ago, the professor told us. That's when they built the strange modern building to replace it. I thought it was an interesting-looking building, I said. Professor Pittman thought it looked like a blushing buzzard with a broken wing (which didn't seem like a very poetic thing to say).

The professor leaned back in his creaky chair. "Now, why would someone as young as you be interested in an artifact like the old library?" he murmured. "I would think such an avocation to be strictly for the old folks . . . say thirty or over!"

The professor chuckled softly at his own joke. Rob and I did too, though to tell you the truth, it was getting a little stale. We had heard it before from Danny . . . and even Mama.

Rob told him about our ancestor's lost invention, and Professor Pittman smiled. "I've always been curious about that myself," he admitted. "I wish you luck, but somehow I doubt that the old apparatus is still around." He studied a pencil which he rolled between his palms. "Apparently it was discarded many years ago; perhaps even before the inventor died."

"But there's still a chance!" Rob argued. "They might have moved it when the old building burned. They could have saved it, you know, and stored it somewhere in the art building . . . an attic or somewhere."

The professor laughed. It was like the wind in dry leaves. "You're John Summerville's grandson, all right! Fiery red hair and a fiery spirit to match!"

Rob squirmed. He was touchy about his red hair. "Did you really know my grandpa?" he asked.

"John was a good bit younger than I was," the professor said, "but I remember him." He was silent a moment, then slowly smiled. "His sister, now, was nearer my age. Perhaps a few years older, but we ambled about in the same social circles. She was a charmer, your Aunt Matilda—a special leh-dy —and many a young man was caught by the sound of her laughter. How she could tear up a piano!" Gray lights danced in his eyes and they crinkled at the corners. "You know, she could have been an accomplished musician if she had taken it seriously."

"Really?" Rob was sitting on the edge of the professor's desk; I shoved him off.

"I believed she could do anything she wanted to," he said, "and she glorified in all of it." His smile faded. "So vibrant a life to have ended so unhappily."

"Do you remember what happened?" I asked. "We found her picture in an old scrapbook in the attic. She was so pretty! It just doesn't seem fair."

He shook his shaggy gray head. "There was an unfortunate romance. Perhaps I shouldn't tell you this, but it can't hurt her now: it was rumored that the young man—ah— embezzled some money, then took his life. . . . " His voice trailed off like the end of a song. I caught myself leaning forward to hear him.

"But he didn't!" Rob shouted. "I just know he didn't!"

The professor seemed startled out of a dream. "Well, it's past history now. I wouldn't dwell on it. Your Aunt Matilda was a delightful young woman, and a happy one until he came along."

He stared out the window for a minute and his eyes had that faraway look, as if he were seeing into the past. "I don't suppose the town will ever forget the time she talked her entire class into playing hooky from school on April Fool's Day. She was a senior in high school then, and I was a year or so behind. I thought she was the most daring, wonderful person in the world!" He chuckled. "Of course they were nearly expelled, but I hear they had an elegant picnic. . . ."

We tiptoed out. The professor was having such a good time remembering, we didn't want to disturb him.

We stood on the steps of the art building for a long time, trying to work up enough courage to go inside. What I really wanted to do was go home and start writing my article about Miss Ida. Fresh ideas were jumping around in my head like crickets, just dying to hop out on paper!

"Let's come back later," I said to Rob. "We really don't know where to look, and besides, I'm tired."

"Oh, no you don't!" he screamed. "You made me come over here, and I wanna know what's in this building!"

A lady stuck her head out of the window of the art building and told us to go away.

We didn't go away, we went inside instead; but there was nobody to help us—except the fussy woman—and we weren't about to let her know we were there.

Finally we ran into the caretaker. He wasn't too pleasant either, but he did grumble that nothing was saved from the old library fire back in 1925 except a few old books and a bust of Plato.

"I was right here when they moved into the new building last year," he bragged. "In fact, I carried a lot of the books. I would have known it if there had been any invention in this building. Why, there wouldn't have been anyplace to put it." He rumbled off down the empty hall, pushing his little cart of mops and brooms. He looked like he enjoyed being able to disappoint us.

We raced out into the sunlight and jumped over the petunia bed in the middle of the walk. I didn't quite make it. Rob sneaked under the window where the lady had shouted at us to go away, and told her good-bye. She slammed the window shut.

I had had enough of King's Creek College for a while, and more than enough of my brother Robert. "Beat you home!" I shouted, remembering a shortcut I had seen that morning. I knew he would tell Danny I had run off and left him when we got home, but it was worth it.

I was still laughing to myself when I turned the corner and ran smack into the judge's soft stomach.

"Oomph!" the judge said as he stumbled backward into a privet hedge; he ended up with his feet in the air. I was getting used to seeing Judge Hardigree in a prone position.

If I could have disappeared into thin air, I would have done it. I guess the judge was beginning to think I was some sort of jinx; maybe I was.

Getting Judge Hardigree out of the privet hedge was like being on the opposite end of a seesaw from a gorilla! The judge even sounded a little like a gorilla with all his snorting and growling. I really felt awful! Mama is always telling me to look where I'm going.

Once he recovered, the judge seemed to take it pretty well. I told him I was sorry about five times and helped him pick up the letters that were scattered all over the sidewalk. He was on his way to the post office, he said, and since we were both headed in the same direction, I walked along with him. I don't think he was particularly thrilled with my company, but there were a few minor details I wanted to worm out of Judge Arthur P. Hardigree, and here was the perfect chance to do it.

I hopped along beside him as if I were just too happy for words. Then I laid a smile on him: sweet and innocent and adoring—like Shirley Temple in the old movies.

"Did you know that you and I could have been kinfolk, Judge?" I glanced up through the tops of my glasses. I'm afraid I don't look very much like Shirley Temple.

The judge stuffed the smudged envelopes into his inside coat pocket. "How is that, my little friend?"

I tried not to cringe at being called his "little friend," and pretended to think. "Well, my Aunt Matilda was engaged to one of your relatives. Your uncle, I think."

"Aunt Matilda? Don't believe I remember her. My uncle, you say?"

"Your Uncle Calvin; and actually, it was my Great-Aunt Matilda. She died, though. They both did, a long time ago." I waited.

Judge Hardigree wiped his face with a balled-up handkerchief and looked like he was holding his breath for a moment. "Ah, yes, well, that was a long time ago. Before I came into this old world, if you can believe that!"

I smiled at his joke. "Doesn't it bother you that Calvin is buried outside the churchyard?" I asked sweetly.

The judge began to walk faster. He pretended not to hear me. "I said, doesn't it bother you about Calvin not being buried in the family plot?" I repeated, hurrying to catch up. "He was your uncle, wasn't he?"

Finally he stopped and gave me a quick, fatherly pat. (I was glad for the rest; the judge can walk pretty fast for a fat guy.) "I know you mean well, my dear," he said, "but there are some things better left alone. I never knew my Uncle Calvin; I never knew your Great-Aunt Matilda. But I thought highly of your Uncle Zeb, and your great-grandparents. Charming people, yes, indeed. Salt of the earth they were." The judge waved his arms as if he were leading an orchestra.

"Such dear, dear friends, your family," he went on. "Why, I remember your grandfather when—" He stopped with a hand in midair. "Does your grandmother know you're out poking about into other people's affairs? I don't think she'd like that. I don't think she'd like that at all."

I didn't like the judge right then, not even a little bit, but I tried to be polite. Danny would clobber me if I weren't polite. "I know it's not nice to pry," I said, "and I'm sorry, but I do have a good reason!"

I turned and ran, leaving him alone on the hot sidewalk, mopping his face in the sun.

Danny says you can catch more flies with honey than with vinegar, but just then I was feeling more than a little on the sour side. Besides, who wants sticky flies?

CHAPTER 15

The next day started out crummy. It rained and my hair frizzed, and Lucy and I had our first fight . . . or fuss, rather. We didn't actually get to the hitting stage, but I felt like it.

We were walking home from Sunday school together when she invited me to come along for cheering practice that afternoon. She and some of the other girls were getting together to work on their cheers so they would be ready to try out for the junior high team.

"No thanks," I said. "I'd rather clean out the garbage cans. Why do you want to mess around like that, anyway? I can think of a million better things to do."

"Like what?" she asked. "Why do you have this hang-up about cheering, Peggy? You'd like it, really, it's fun."

"It's silly! If you knew how ridiculous you look, jumping around like that—"

Lucy's mouth went tight. "Oh, when are you going grow up and quit trying to be a boy? What's so terrible about being a girl? I like doing girl things—and you'd better learn to, too, 'cause you're stuck with it!"

I really wanted to hurt her then. "Well, maybe I can do a few *other* things better than some people I know. If you want to act like a dummy, go ahead!"

I walked off and left her standing there with her mouth

open, and I hated myself.

As soon as I got home I went up to my room and took my pigtails down. I was the only girl at Saint Luke's with pigtails! I must have brushed my hair for half an hour, trying to get the waves out where the plaits had been.

When Rob came up to call me down for lunch, I wouldn't answer him. They say the weather affects your disposition; well, maybe that's because it affects your hair. Mine was all frizzled out like a grizzly bear's, and the more I brushed it the more it stuck out.

"Peggy?" Mama called at the door and I let her in. There are times when you don't have to explain things to mothers; at least I don't. Mama took the brush and smoothed my hair back in a ponytail. It didn't look so bad. Still, I wish it were straight and smooth like Lucy's. When Lucy turns her head, her hair goes with it. When I turn my head, my hair goes in about ten different directions!

Mama sat down beside me and gave me a hug. "It looks like a Brillo pad," I cried, "and it feels like one too!"

She pulled my head down on her shoulder. "It's time we had it cut. I'll make an appointment tomorrow."

I felt a little better then, sort of.

"Something's bothering you besides your hair, isn't it, Peggy?" Mama asked finally.

Then I told her about Lucy and the cheerleading: what I had done. "I don't have to like things like that, do I?" I asked. "Just because I'm a girl? I'm not very good at looking cute and being graceful! Does it really matter all that much?"

Mama gave me a quick kiss. "Of course not. Everybody has her own talents, and that's the way it should be. You have a quick wit and a way with words, and I'm proud of you. I wouldn't want you to change."

I wiped my eyes. "That's because you're my mother."

She laughed. "Well, possibly, but wouldn't it be dull if we were all alike? That's why you should never belittle anyone else's talents. I imagine you've hurt Lucy, and if you really care about her as I think you do, you'll tell her you're sorry.

The sooner the better."

"But what if she doesn't want to make up?"

Mama smiled. "She will, you wait and see."

It was still dripping outside after lunch and it didn't help my day any. "April showers bring May flowers," Danny said. I guess August showers bring goldenrod.

I wanted to go over to Lucy's, but I was afraid she wouldn't speak to me, so I put it off some more and found a good book to read. It was *Huckleberry Finn*, which is one of my favorites. I've read it twice already, but it was good for another round, and even more. The old daybed that had been Aunt Jane's made a cozy nook for reading in the upstairs hall, and I was into the fourth chapter when I heard a car door slam in the driveway and Sunday voices on the porch.

I jumped up, ready to hide because I just knew it was Judge Hardigree come to tell Danny how nosy I had been. But it was Joel's voice I heard in the downstairs hall. I practically melted with relief.

I left Huck having a conversation with Judge Thatcher and ran down to find Joel. He wanted to know all about my interview with Miss Ida, so we sat out on the back steps and I told him about it while he played with Animal.

He didn't seem too surprised that Miss Ida had seen our ghost too. And he laughed so hard when I told him about the peppermint urn, that Mama, Danny, and a strange man came out to ask what was so funny.

The man turned out to be Joel's father. He looked so much like Joel, I think I could have guessed who he was even if they hadn't introduced us. They were both tall and loose and gray-eyed.

Joel's father took us all to dinner that night, so my day wasn't a complete disaster. Of course Danny put up her usual fuss and insisted that they eat there with us, but for once she had to give in to somebody who could argue better than she could.

When I told Joel that Miss Ida needed a gardener, he kind of took to the idea. I think he was glad to have something to do. He was saving up to buy a stereo, he said, and the money would help, no matter how little it was.

"What about the invention?" he asked later as we were driving home from the restaurant. "Did you find out anything more about that?"

We told him about our visit with Professor Pittman and the crabby janitor in the art building, but I didn't say anything about running into the judge—not with Danny there in the same car.

"I don't know, but I feel like we've wound up at a dead end," I said. "It looks like the invention just disappeared; maybe it was burned in the fire. I just don't know where else to look. And what are we going to do about Aunt Matilda?" I added in a whisper.

Joel looked gloomy too. "Well, at least we know who Calvin was. There must be some way we can get them to move his grave."

"Well, what else does she expect us to do? Go out and dig him up?"

"There must be something," Joel said, "something we don't know. I don't think we've seen the last of Aunt Matilda."

We played croquet until it got too dark, and then Joel brought over his guitar and we sat on the front porch with the grown-ups and sang. Joel could play just about anything we asked him to, but he was really good on "Jeremiah Was a Bullfrog." Rob made him play it four times.

It was peaceful on the porch in the dark with the voices and the music and the summer night noises. I curled up in the big wicker chair and closed my eyes. I felt safe and contented and happy—almost. I wished Lucy could have been there too, like we were before we had our fuss.

I wonder if God ever lets you get completely happy. Maybe He's afraid you'll get mixed-up and think you're in heaven.

CHAPTER 16

WHAM! WHACK! I woke up to a terrible noise! It sounded like somebody was tearing the house down, and it was coming from Rob's room. He wouldn't let me in. "The atom bomb has already been invented," I called through the door . . . no answer. I guess we have a communication gap.

I shoved down my breakfast and headed for Lucy's. No more "putting off," or procrastinating, as Danny calls it. By the time I got to her house, I began to back down a little. After all, it hadn't been *all* my fault. Oh well, somebody had to begin.

She was cleaning her room, her mother said. She looked up when I came in and kind of grinned. She was glad to see me, I think. There was a big box in front of her, stacked to the top with layers and layers of Barbie clothes.

"I'm giving them away." She shrugged. "I guess I'm getting too big."

I sat on the bed. "Lucy, I feel awful about what I said yesterday. I really didn't mean it."

She stuffed some more clothes in the box. "I know. I do too, and I'm sorry. It bothered me all day. Mother told me I shouldn't expect everyone to be just like me."

I laughed. "So did mine!"

Then I knew everything was going to be okay.

"Peggy, you be you, and I'll be me. Let's just keep on being friends."

I agreed. "It's just that I'm not good at cheering," I said. "My hair gets all in my face and my glasses fall off. I feel like I do everything wrong. I would like to learn one thing, though."

"Sure, what's that?"

"I've always wanted to know how to turn a cartwheel."

"Okay, I'll teach you—this afternoon, if I ever get this room straight."

"Look for me in the summerhouse," I told her as I left. "I have to get started on that feature story before I forget all the facts."

Rob was still bumping around in his room and Danny was in a letter-writing mood, so I took my notes from the interview with Miss Ida back in the woods. It was good to have a place where I could get away by myself and think.

In the gray-green quiet of the summerhouse, I began to put the pieces together, and finally my story was finished. It was good, much better than my usual stuff.

I even concocted an advice column: I called it "Bessie Mae Blunose." It wasn't a real advice column, of course. The letters were from characters like Long John Silver, who was having a problem with termites in his leg; and from Marie Antoinette, who wanted to know how to get *ahead* in life. I knew I should have had some kind of article about school registration, but it was too grim to think about.

Animal was making a game out of collecting all kinds of junk from the woods and piling it in the middle of the floor. So far he had found an empty bread wrapper, an old ham bone, a rusty fruit jar lid, and two crushed beer cans. Maybe he's really a retriever. The only thing missing was my yellow pencil with the good eraser on it.

Joel was his usual, timely self, making his appearance just before lunch. He read my story on Miss Ida and actually said it was good! He thought the advice column was "yellow journalism."

"I don't care what color it is," I told him. "Kids like stuff like that; it sells papers."

"You don't have to cheapen your paper with junk like that," he argued. "At least try to make it look classy."

"Well, what's wrong with it? It's cute. I like it."

"Cute!" he snorted. "Sure it's cute! But newspapers aren't supposed to be cute. You just don't need it, that's all. Take it out, Peggy."

That did it. "It's *my* paper and it stays in! What makes you think you know so much about running a paper, anyway?"

He kicked one of Animal's rusty treasures with the toe of his shoe. "I worked on the school paper before we came here. Besides, I read a lot."

He was really beginning to get to me. I wondered if there were *anything* I could do even a little bit better than somebody else. "I read a lot, too," I said.

Joel didn't answer. He picked up something from the weird pile on the floor and turned it over in his hand. It was bright, not like the rest of the junk. He held it up to the light. "Hey, look! It's a tiepin. Wonder where it came from?"

"Where did you find it?"

"It just fell out of this can. But how in the world did it get in there?"

The pin had a design of three rectangles, each one inside a larger one. It seemed familiar, but anybody might have one like it. It was a simple design.

"I think I've seen this before," I said, "but I can't remember where."

"Maybe it's Dad's," Joel said. "He has one kinda like this."

I dropped the pin in the pocket of my shorts. "I'll ask Danny. Maybe she'll know." I decided to forget our journalistic differences—for the time being, anyway. "How does a sandwich sound to you?" I asked.

Joel grinned. "I thought you'd never ask!"

Rob didn't come down for lunch. He was still playing the part of the dedicated, hermit-like inventor guarding his great discovery. I guess he ate lunch in his room: probably a crust of stale bread or something noble like that. Danny was eating some kind of diet stuff, so she didn't have lunch with us, either. It was just Joel and me. We fixed some sandwiches and ate them out on the back porch.

Joel was different from other boys; usually I don't know what to say around boys my own age. I either feel silly and talk too much, or I can't think of a thing to say. It was easy talking to Joel. I liked him, even if he was bossy. He really did have some good ideas about the paper; he even said he'd ask his dad if he would run it off for us on the copy machine in his office. But there was a lot of work to be done before we got to the printing stage, Joel said. We needed to get organized.

Well, if there's one thing I'm allergic to, it's getting organized. I reckon I hate it almost as much as cheering, but this time I knew he was right. We got organized.

Lucy came over after lunch and was given the gruesome job of writing up school registration. She was also made circulation manager, since she knew the most people. We were going to ask Rob to be the paper carrier, but we never figured out a tactful way to do it.

Lucy thought my advice column was the greatest. She even wanted me to make it longer, but I didn't; I knew when I was ahead.

She drew a crazy one-panel cartoon of the comic strip character Batman on the beach in a bathing suit. He was white everywhere his suit and mask had been; only his face was tan. The name of the comic was "What If?" and underneath she had written, "What makes you think I'm Batman?" Even Joel liked it, but he said it would be better with the punch line left out. "Everybody will know he's Batman anyway. You don't need it," he explained.

So we took it out, and he was right: it *was* funnier . . . but Bessie Mae Blunose stayed.

The paper was beginning to shape up. Joel took care of sports and layout, and I covered the rest of the news. I was trying to think of a good headline for my lead story when my brother finally came out of hiding.

We were working out in the summerhouse when he came plowing through the bushes, yelling and shouting and scaring everybody half to death. Even Animal ran!

"It's ready! Come and see it!" Those round, brown eyes of his looked as if they might pop right out of his head, and he didn't wait for us to follow him, but took off up the path, yelling for us to come on.

We put the articles we had been working on in a cardboard box and anchored them down with a rock. Even if it rained, they would keep dry in the summerhouse, and nobody would bother them there—we thought.

By the time we got to the house, my side was aching. Rob had rigged two pulleys at the side of the house under his window. One was fastened outside his upstairs window frame with a double cord reaching down to another pulley a few feet from the ground. And . . . get this . . . hanging from the lower pulley on a hook was the bottom part of that old baby carriage we had found in the basement, minus the wheels!

Everybody just stood there and stared at it. Nobody said a word; it was hard to think of something to say.

Finally I couldn't stand it any longer. "What is it?"

He shook his head at such a stupid question. "You are looking at the Lazy Day Manual Rotary Machine," he said. "Or in plain language, a hand-operated basket elevator."

Lucy looked suspicious. "What does it elevate?"

"Anything, as long as it's not too heavy. I'm gonna use it to carry stuff upstairs. I thought I'd try it out on Animal if I can catch him."

"Oh, no you're not!" I yelled. "What if the rope breaks or something? Besides, you'll never get him in it."

He looked at me like Julius Caesar must have looked at Brutus. "It's perfectly safe. Here, I'll show you."

He picked up a few bricks from the border around the flower bed and put them in the basket. When he pulled on the loose end of the rope, the basket moved to the top without a hitch.

Sometimes he was a pain in the neck, but he was my brother and I was proud of him. "Wow, you've finally come up with something that works," I said. "That's really neat, Rob."

He turned a bright shade of pink and grinned. "I might even get a patent on it."

Joel was looking kind of funny. "I hate to be the one to tell you, Rob, but the block and tackle has already been invented."

Rob just looked at him. I wanted to put my arm around my brother, but I knew better. "Oh," he said. "Is that what you call it?"

Joel nodded. "It's been around a long time; you've probably seen one somewhere . . . but yours is a good one. It really is a good block and tackle, Robert. You did a professional job on it."

Rob shrugged. "Oh, well, there are plenty of other things left to invent, and I can still use this. Think of the trouble it will save!"

He was being such a good sport about it, I decided to take a chance and let Animal ride in the Lazy Day Manual Rotary Machine. But I stood underneath it, ready to catch him—just in case.

Animal had his mind made up about riding in that basket: he was not going to do it. Finally we got him in by bribing him with the ham bone Danny was saving for her soup. Animal really went after that bone! In fact, he was so busy gnawing on it that he didn't realize he had been for a ride until the basket started back down. Then he whimpered a little. After that Animal expected a goodie every time he rode in the elevator, and he always got one.

After we got tired of playing with the elevator, Lucy invited us over to her house for homemade ice cream. We stayed to roast hot dogs for supper and it was late when we got home. I forgot to ask Danny about the gold tiepin. In fact, I didn't think any more about it until it turned up in the washing machine a few days later.

CHAPTER 17

A curious thing happened while we were getting the paper ready for print. It was the day after Joel had found the tiepin; only the tiepin was at the bottom of the laundry hamper in the pocket of my dirty shorts, and I had forgotten all about it.

Joel had gone over to Miss Ida's to tackle her rose garden, so Lucy and I went down to the summerhouse to see how many stories we could squeeze in on four sheets of typing paper. Most of the stories were finished, but there was still some cutting and polishing to do.

I was in a hurry to get our papers out of the box and get to work; maybe some of Joel's organizing had rubbed off on me. But the papers weren't in the box: they were everywhere! On the floor, under the steps, in the bushes—everywhere! And they were dirty and torn and messy. Most of them would have to be written over.

I just stood there and stared. I felt like somebody had yanked out my bones, like I was hollow inside.

Lucy let out a yell, not a dainty little cheerleader yell, but a regular down-in-the-stomach holler. "I thought you said you put a rock on the box!"

We scrambled around on our hands and knees, trying to pick them all up. "I did! I know I did, and it was a big rock, too. There it is over there . . . at the foot of the steps. Lucy, how did it get there?"

"A dog must have gotten in it," she said, crawling across the floor to grab the last crinkled sheet. "I think it's all here, though."

"Dog, my foot!" I argued. "A dog would have knocked over the box. Besides, why would a dog lift off that rock, carry it down the steps, take out all the papers, and throw them on the floor?"

She giggled. "Maybe it didn't like what we wrote."

It didn't look like I was going to get any help from Lucy. It really bothered me that somebody would do such a mean, hateful thing to our newspaper, and it wasn't a bit of fun having to worry about it all by myself. Joel was supposed to stop by for the stories on his way home from Miss Ida's, and I wished he would hurry. Maybe he would have some idea who had made this mess.

But Joel wasn't in any mood for mysteries. He was tired and sweaty and thirsty, with grass sticking to him and ugly gashes from thorns all over his arms. Danny felt sorry for him and made him a pitcher of iced tea. He drank the whole thing.

Lucy and I had managed to rewrite the damaged articles before he came by, and I felt tired and crabby—like you are when you get in too much of a hurry. "I don't guess it matters to you who messed up our papers," I said. "You didn't have to write them over!"

"It was probably just the wind." He shrugged. "Are you sure you put the rock on that box, Peggy?"

I didn't even bother to answer.

"Oh, well," said Lucy the peacemaker, "what does it matter? We got all our stories back, didn't we?"

I pretended to forget it, but I knew the wind hadn't scattered those papers, or a dog either . . . and so did Joel.

I was over my "mad," though, by the time our issue of *The Leader* came out—and happy enough to forgive everybody. It was really something special, and worth every minute of the work we had put into it. I was kind of glad old bossy Joel had been such a perfectionist—only I wouldn't tell him that.

Mama designed the masthead in Old English letters, and underneath we printed the slogan: "Follow The Leader." (Joel said that was just too, too cute for words.) He typed the pages on an old typewriter of his dad's, and Professor Henderson ran off about fifty copies on the copy machine in the history department. Everybody liked my story about Miss Ida, especially Miss Ida. She even liked "Bessie Mae Blunose"; said it was the best thing in the whole paper! I was so proud of *The Leader*, I slept with a copy under my pillow for a week after it came out.

Lucy and I decided to combine business with pleasure a few days later and unload some papers at the pool. It turned out to be a great idea because we sold almost every copy we had.

"Just think, there won't be many more days of swimming left," Lucy reminded me as we rested from our last race. "I hate to miss a day of it, but we've gotta go pick up Evelyn at camp this weekend."

"Oh, no! Lucy, you've just got to stay here this weekend! I just know something's gonna happen Saturday night, about Aunt Matilda, I mean."

"How, come? What's special about Saturday night?"

"Don't you remember? I told you, Danny and Mama are giving this dinner party for Judge Hardigree and Miss Ida. I think they're going to ask Joel and his dad too. You wouldn't want to miss that, would you?"

She looked sick. "You know I wouldn't, but what can I do? My folks are planning to stay overnight with some friends on the way back and make sort of a vacation out of it." She groaned. "Maybe they won't make me go."

"You can stay with us. I'll get Danny to call and invite you if it'll help."

Lucy grinned. "It will. It just has to!" She flopped on her stomach to give the sun a chance to even up her honey-colored tan.

I sat in the sun, letting my feet swish in the water while about a million freckles popped out on my hide, but I didn't care. My hair was shaggy and wet, but I knew it would curl just enough when it dried. Already a few of the girls I had met at Sunday school had told me it looked cute cut short, and I kinda liked it, too. At least, when I looked in the mirror, I didn't want to go hide in the closet.

Lucy and I spent the next few days getting ready for the weekend. Danny must have really done a snow job on Lucy's parents, because they agreed to let her stay without any fuss at all. I said it was because Danny was such a diplomat; Lucy said she thought maybe her folks were just a little bit glad to get rid of her for a while.

We were sitting at the kitchen table the Thursday before the weekend, making out a schedule for Friday. We hardly ever followed any of the plans we made, but it was fun thinking them up. Anyway, before I knew it, Danny was peeping over my shoulder, reading every word! She was grinning all over. "Do you have a special time to go to the bathroom?" she asked.

I slammed my hand over the paper so she couldn't read any more, but it was too late. She wandered off, shaking her head. "Why bother to close the barn door after the horse is stolen?" she laughed.

She wouldn't think it was so funny when she found out we were keeping Rover for the weekend, too. Danny can't stand cats.

CHAPTER 18

Lucy's dad brought her over the next day with enough stuff to last until Christmas. She had Rover in a cardboard box, her suitcase, three pairs of shoes, and something that looked like a violin case. I found out later that it really was a violin case, complete with a violin. After I'd heard her play, I wished I'd never found out at all! Danny said she would rather listen to the cat.

We let the cat out of the box to make friends with Animal and found a flat, grassy spot in the backyard for me to practice cartwheels. I needed more than grass to fall on; I needed a mattress, but I was getting a little better. It was easier having short hair; at least I could see where I was supposed to be going.

"Jeremiah was a bullfrog!" Rob bellowed. He was upstairs in his room with his window open, probably working on another great advancement in science—like the wheel.

Lucy did a running cartwheel under his window. "What is it this time?" she hooted. "The telephone or the sewing machine?"

Rob came to the window and grinned. He liked Lucy. "Something new. Wait'll you see it!"

"I'm holding my breath," Lucy laughed.

We rested under the pecan tree, chewing on cinnamon

toothpicks and planning for Saturday. The days were getting shorter and August would soon be over. I hated for it to end; sometimes I think it would be fun if we could hold time still, like in a photograph. Then there are other times when I know it's not such a great idea.

We heard the front gate shut and the tapping of the judge's cane on the walk. I could tell he was swinging it by the way it missed the ground every other step.

Plunk . . . swish . . . plunk . . . swish. . . . We spied on him from the side of the house and saw him stop at the bottom porch step. He stepped *over* it!

We hid in the bushes and giggled. Lucy doubled over, shaking, and poked me with her elbow.

I flattened myself against the side of the house and held my breath to keep from laughing out loud. Finally the front door opened and shut. "Old fatso!" I said. "Wish he'd stay at home!"

"You'd better be nice to him," Lucy teased. "He might just be our next state senator. Besides, if he marries Danny, he'll probably move in with you. You'll have to see him every day!"

"Yuck! Over my dead body!" I groaned.

Lucy flipped her feet in the air in a long, lazy handstand and came up with grass in her hair. "Speaking of bodies," she said. "Do you think we'll see Aunt Matilda tonight?"

"I don't think so, not unless she has something to tell us. But just wait until tomorrow!"

And I was right. We didn't see Aunt Matilda that night. Danny went out somewhere with Judge Hardigree, and Mama treated Lucy, Rob, and me to hamburgers and a movie. It was getting late when we got back home, so we went right to bed. Lucy and I took turns listening for Aunt Matilda in case she decided to drop in, but the only visitor we had was Rover, who pounced on the bed and curled into a sleeping ball between us. Danny would have had a fit . . . but we didn't tell her.

The next thing I knew I was dreaming of a dragon: a snarling, growling dragon with a fat stomach and square-rimmed glasses. I knew I was dreaming because dragons aren't for real—I don't think. Besides, this one was wearing a smushed hat with a dead rose in it. "Help me! Help me!" it howled.

In the morning I sat straight up in bed and glared at my mother, who was thumping the vacuum sweeper under by bed. Lucy covered her face with the sheet. "What is it?" she mumbled.

"Time to get up!" Mama commanded. "There's too much to do to lie in bed today." She jerked off my sheet. "Up! Up and at 'em!"

I flopped on my belly and shoved by head under the pillow. "Quit it! Leave me alone!"

The pillow went flying. "Out!" Mama said. She meant business.

We were given French toast and bacon for breakfast—and ten minutes to eat it. Danny was in a hurry to get through in the kitchen. Rob had already eaten and was out sweeping the walk. I could tell he was griping because his face was red. "Get ready," I told Lucy. "They'll find a job for us, too." And sure enough, they did. But it really didn't matter. We seemed to be in somebody's way, no matter where we went. At least we could pretend to be busy.

We drew the disagreeable chore of cleaning the parakeet's cage. The parakeet's name was Oscar, and he wasn't the brightest bird in the world. I spent practically a whole morning once trying to teach him to talk, but he never learned a word.

Danny keeps his cage in the playroom where he does nothing all day except ruffle his pretty blue feathers and throw seeds on the floor. Danny thinks he's adorable. We only had to change the paper in the bottom of the cage and put fresh water in his dish, so it didn't take long. Danny checked us out from the kitchen door. "Remember, anything worth doing is worth doing well," she said.

We finished Oscar's housecleaning and slipped back upstairs to listen to music for a while. Danny was in the kitchen making one of her broccoli-onion casseroles that everybody loves—everybody but me, that is, but she always makes me take one bite to "develop my sense of taste." Danny says I have immature taste buds. If it takes broccoli to develop them, they'll just have to stay that way!

Lucy had brought over her newest tape and we had played it about five times when Mama knocked at my door.

"I don't care how many times you play that thing," she told us, "only not so loud, please!" Mama put her hands over her ears. "I'm not ready for a hearing aid yet."

I was trying to keep a straight face. "Eh? What'd you say? I can't hear you."

We were tired of hearing the same thing too, so we turned off the tape player and dug up the Ouija board to see if we could communicate with Aunt Matilda. Either Aunt Matilda was asleep, or she didn't have anything to say, because the pointer didn't budge an inch. When Rob is my partner, the pointer jumps all over the place. The only trouble is, it spells like a ten-year-old.

We gave up after ten minutes. "Oh, come on," I said. "Aunt Matilda doesn't need a Ouija. She can reach us by herself. Let's see what Rob's doing. Maybe we can look some more for the invention. There must be someplace around here we've missed."

But Rob was busy with an invention of his own. He did let us in his room, though, so he could show Lucy his hamsters, Grits and Gravy.

Hamsters would be kind of pretty if they didn't look so much like rats. They're soft and fuzzy, brownish-gold, and friendly, too, in a hamster sort of way.

Lucy took one of them out of its cage and let it run up her arm. It made me shudder! Grits and Gravy are both boys. The first Gravy was a girl, but she died after having about fifty babies. (Not all at once!) Danny said she died from exhaustion. Anyway, Rob sold all the babies to a pet shop, except for one to keep his daddy company. Now I couldn't tell them apart, but Rob could.

He was working on a burglar alarm for his room, and the hamsters were part of the invention. He showed us how it worked. There was a string connecting his doorknob to the latch on the hamster's cage. When somebody opened the door, the hamsters were released into a sort of passageway made of an old washboard and Mama's biscuit pan. At the end of the passage was a shoe box which worked on weights. The wildest thing about it was that the weight was Danny's old dinner bell. The weight of the hamsters made the shoe box glide to the floor, while the bell at the other end of the string rose clanging in the air.

It was crazy. Definitely the work of a mad inventor.

"Why don't you just hang the bell from your doorknob?" I asked. "Wouldn't that be a lot easier?"

I shouldn't have asked. My brother's expression put me at the bottom of the idiot class. "Well, *that* wouldn't be any fun," he said.

Lucy and I were hoping that Joel would come early and bring his guitar, but Rob said he was playing softball with a bunch of boys down at the park, so I knew we wouldn't see him until supper.

Danny let us set the table in the big dining room with our best china and silver and the crystal candelabra that had been her mother's. Miss Ida had sent armloads of roses by Joel earlier that morning, and they made the whole house seem special. When I'm grown and give dinner parties of my own, I'm always going to have flowers on the table. But I'm not going to have broccoli.

Danny had to remind Lucy to practice her violin, but I don't think she wanted to. Danny has a strong constitution. I made my shower last for as long as the screeching went on and used up most of the hot water.

Somehow we were all ready before time for everybody to come, and I was getting nervous. What if Judge Hardigree told Mama and Danny what I had done? I wouldn't put it past him, but I didn't think he would say anything tonight. At least not until after dinner. Still, my stomach was squirming when the doorbell rang, and wouldn't you know—it was the judge! He brought along another bunch of roses which he soon learned we didn't need, but Danny fussed over them anyway. He tried not to look at me and I tried not to look at him, and I ended up getting a crick in my neck.

I was glad when Joel and his dad came in with Miss Ida a few minutes later. Then we had to wait while the grown-ups had drinks and hors d'oeuvres in the parlor. Mama calls them hors d'oeuvres; they look like cheese and crackers to me.

After a few minutes of polite chatter, we finally filed into the dining room. I was glad to get to the eating part.

Miss Ida smiled at Mama over the frozen fruit salad. "You've certainly done a lot with this house," she said. "I'm afraid poor Zeb let it go when his health got so bad."

"A charming home for two such charming ladies. By the way," the judge began casually with his salad fork in midair, "Have you come across that old diary of Zeb's? He was our family friend and physician for many, many years, you see, and he—well, he mentioned once that he wanted me to have it."

Miss Ida gave him a funny look. "That's odd. I never noticed your being so close."

The judge turned a shade pinker. "Well—harumph— Doctor Zeb was nearer my father's age, of course; but being neighbors, we naturally saw a great deal of each other."

Danny seemed kind of confused by it all. "Well, if the diary is here, you should have it, by all means." She turned to Mama. "You haven't run across it, have you, dear?"

"It could be anywhere," Mama admitted. "Thomas left most of the old books, and some furniture too. I guess he doesn't have room for it all."

"I cleaned those shelves in the parlor and dusted the books before we moved in," Danny told him, "but I don't remember seeing a diary. I guess my eyesight isn't as good as it used to be. It's probably around here somewhere; if it is, I'll find it."

The judge flashed her a smile calculated to melt a polar ice cap. "My most kind and generous lady, how can I ever thank you enough?" He turned to include the rest of us, spreading his goodwill around the table. "What ever would we do without our dear friends, I wonder?"

He waved his napkin like a banner; I halfway expected him to jump up on his chair and begin a speech, but as he caught my eye the napkin disappeared under the table. I was disappointed.

"Well, if it does happen to turn up," he said, "I would like to have it. Its value lies solely in the sentiment, of course." He stuffed a glob of broccoli in his mouth.

I felt a mean spell coming on. I guess I ought to learn to leave well enough alone, as Danny says, but just being around the judge did something to me. "By the way," I said loudly, "I was just telling the judge the other day that we were almost kin." I helped myself to another roll and passed them to Lucy with a jab of my elbow.

Miss Ida had a wicked gleam in her eye. "Why, of course! You and the judge would have been cousins, wouldn't you? That is, if your Great-Aunt Matilda had married Calvin Hardigree. Or is it cousins-in-law?" she added in a puzzled voice. "Did you ever have Calvin's grave moved, Judge?"

The judge seemed to be having a hard time swallowing . . . probably the broccoli. "I'm afraid there's not much I can do about that, Miss Ida," he muttered.

"Who in the world was Calvin Hardigree?" Mama asked, looking surprised. "And what's this about a grave?"

The judge didn't answer, and from the look on his face we could tell he wasn't going to.

"Won't you have some more chicken, Miss Ida?" Danny offered. We got on with our eating.

It was while we were having dessert that I suddenly remembered the gold tiepin. Joel's dad was sitting across from me, and the reflection of the candle flame on the pin he wore reminded me of the other one, the one in the pocket of my shorts.

"Hey, I almost forgot," I said, "Joel and I found a tiepin

down by the—"

"If you mean the one that went through the washing machine, it's the cleanest pin in town," Danny interrupted. "Where did you find that, Peggy? It must belong to one of you two men since you're the only tie-wearers who've been here recently."

"I don't think I've lost one." Joel's dad glanced down at the one he wore. "What does it look like?"

Danny nodded at me. "Run in the kitchen and get it. It's in that catchall jar on the windowsill."

"Why—harumph—yes, I believe that is mine," the judge patted my head as I handed him the pin. "It must have slipped off in a chair somewhere. Or did you find it in the yard?"

I looked at Joel and his eyes said, *No.*

"Oh, it was out in back somewhere," I said.

As Judge Hardigree was reaching for the pin, his shirt cuff had accidentally brushed against the meringue on top of his pie. "Oh, now look what a mess I've made! How clumsy! I'd better go and wash this off before I get it on anything else."

Lucy looked at me out of the sides of her eyes and I wanted to giggle. I thought the judge would never leave the room. He did though, finally; we heard him creaking up the stairs. I couldn't hold the giggles in any longer! They spread from me to Lucy to Rob, and finally to Joel, who was really trying to act dignified. Mama made us go out on the porch.

It was still light enough to play ball, but we didn't want to leave the porch. We were afraid we'd miss something. We sat on the steps while the grown-ups had coffee in the parlor. It seemed as if we had been out there for ages. Maybe we weren't going to have any excitement after all.

Finally Joel unfolded himself from the steps. "I sure would like to have another piece of that lemon pie," he said, "but I'd die before I'd ask for it."

I laughed. "There's more in the kitchen. Come on, we'll go through the hall."

The voices coming from the parlor sounded sleepy and

dull. I was glad we didn't have to sit in there and be bored to death. The others must have been thinking that, too, because they were trying to be extra quiet as we tiptoed past the door. Nobody wanted to be invited in.

We had almost reached the kitchen when it happened. Suddenly everybody started yelling at once, and it was coming from the parlor!

CHAPTER 19

I looked up expecting to see Aunt Matilda floating down the dark hall stairs, and shivered at the thought of the chilling cold she brings. But the house was August-hot and the stairs were bare. I sniffed. The only flower smell around was one of fresh, living roses.

The screaming got louder. *Well, here it comes,* I thought; *the family ghost is at it again!* We raced toward the noise, stepping all over each other's feet. But at the parlor door we stopped.

If we had seen a ghost chasing everyone around the room, I don't think we would have been surprised; or at least I wouldn't. What we did see froze us into one shocked lump.

Danny was jumping around on the sofa *with her shoes on!* Joel's dad was crawling in circles on the floor, and the judge was having some kind of fit, squirming and wiggling, and getting redder and redder! Mama was laughing.

"I've got one!" Professor Henderson yelled, and his big hand reached out for something that moved, something small and golden brown.

"Hey, that's my hamster!" Rob shouted. "How did he get down here?"

"There's another one somewhere." Danny sounded worried. She looked under the sofa. "Hurry, Lucy, catch your cat before she finds it!"

For the first time since we heard the screaming, I noticed Rover, claws out, ready to pounce.

"Oh, no!" Lucy scooped up the kitten just as the hamster darted under the judge's chair. Rover hissed and squirmed, fighting mad, but Lucy hung on. And it was lucky she did, for there was a screeching blue blur and Oscar twitted at us from the mantelpiece, pecking at Mama's Wedgwood vase! Mama stopped laughing.

Rob was feeling under Judge Hardigree's chair for his other hamster when the judge let out a squawk. A strange shudder came over him and a small, furry head with two beady eyes poked from his coat pocket!

That was too much. I sat down on the floor and laughed until the tears poured down my face. Then everybody else started laughing; even the judge managed a weak little smile. I wondered for a while if I would ever be able to stop. Would I grow old laughing? The thought made me giggle even more.

Then the room got quiet: really quiet, like when the school principal comes in the room. I heard a gentle breath of laughter. It grew louder.

Danny looked at me and frowned. So did Mama. I must have looked guilty, but I wasn't the one who was laughing. It seemed to vibrate, as if someone were laughing into a fan. Then it faded, and the room seemed more silent than ever.

The judge began to make excuses about leaving. He gathered his hat and cane in record-breaking time and hopped out the door like a fat Uncle Wiggily. Everybody was so confused, I don't think anyone even noticed he had gone, except for Miss Ida, and she winked at me.

Joel and his dad stayed to help us get our animals back in their cages, and Lucy put Rover in his box for safekeeping. It was like cleaning up after a circus.

"But how did my hamsters get way down here?" Rob wailed as Mama closed the door behind the last guest.

Danny was collecting empty coffee cups. Her hands were shaking. "I told you to keep that cage door shut! At first I thought they were rats." She shuddered.

Rob bit his lip. "But I *did* shut the gate! I know I did."

"He did, Danny," I said. "I saw him. Lucy did, too."

"Well then, how did they manage to get out? And that cat, Margaret; you promised to keep that cat in your room!"

Lucy frowned. "I know we shut the door. I can't imagine how Rover got out."

Mama put her arm around Lucy. "It's all right, don't worry about it," she laughed. "It was almost worth it to me, seeing the judge with that hamster in his pocket!"

"I still don't see how Grits and Gravy got downstairs unless somebody let them out," Rob said. "It couldn't have been one of us. We were all outside."

"He's right," Lucy agreed. "Why, nobody even went upstairs tonight except—"

"Except the judge," I said.

"What's done is done!" Danny snapped off the parlor lights. "And no one's any worse for it, so run on up to bed now and get some sleep. Remember what Benjamin Franklin said: 'Early to bed, and early to rise—'"

"Makes a bullfrog swallow flies!" Rob giggled.

Danny let him have it with a sofa pillow. "Oh, go on!" she said, but she was laughing.

"Well, so much for my burglar alarm," Rob said later. He disconnected the strings from his doorknob. "It didn't even work! See, the shoe box never dropped to the floor. That's why we didn't hear the bell ring."

Lucy stared at the contraption. "Well, it was a good try," she said. "But I guess the hamsters just jumped down the quickest way they could. Rover must have gotten in here somehow."

Rob nodded. "Yeah, and I think I know how."

Lucy poked her finger through the cage to stroke Gravy's little dark head. "But what about Oscar? The judge couldn't have let him out. He didn't even go in the playroom, did he?"

I thought for a minute. "I'll bet I know who did!"

"Who?" Lucy frowned.

I grinned. "Oh, just somebody who likes a joke."

"You mean you think it was Aunt Matilda?" Lucy stared at me, not really believing. "What makes you think she did it?"

I shrugged. "Who else?"

Rob stuck his head out the door and looked down the hall. "Are Mama and Danny still in the kitchen?"

"You know they are," I told him. "Danny never leaves dishes overnight. Besides, I heard her tell Mama she's having her book club here for lunch tomorrow."

Rob shoved open his window. "Then I guess it's safe to haul Animal upstairs." He threw a dog biscuit down into the wicker basket and gave a low whistle.

Animal was curious. He was also hungry. He was always hungry. We watched him waddle from his bed on the back porch and sniff in the basket.

"Get in, boy," Rob ordered. The puppy wagged his tail for a minute while he made up his mind, then climbed in after the biscuit.

"What's Danny going to say if she finds Animal up here?" I asked. "You know she doesn't like dogs in the house."

The basket swayed to the top of the pulley and bumped against the windowsill. Rob lifted out a happy armful of fur and sent the basket on its way. "Why not? I've been doing it all week."

I gave Animal a good-night pat. "Well, suit yourself. I'm not going to share the blame. Come on, Lucy, let's get outta here."

"Do you think Judge Hardigree was the one who let the hamsters out?" Lucy asked as we were getting ready for bed.

"Who else could it have been?" I made a big deal out of clearing my throat. "'Harumph . . . my dear friends . . . how very kind' . . . blah! The old goat! He must have been up here snooping around. He probably didn't even notice he let the cat out."

"I'll bet the hamsters were a surprise!" Lucy laughed.

"What do you think he was looking for?"

"I don't know. That diary of Uncle Zeb's, maybe. He seems awfully anxious to get it. Wonder why?"

Lucy sat in the middle of the bed and brushed her yellow hair; one-two-three-four, it floated up to meet the brush. Mine never floats like that. Suddenly she stopped brushing and looked at me as if I weren't there. "You know, Peg," she said finally, "I'll just bet Judge Hardigree got the meringue on his cuff on purpose!"

I had to admit I hadn't thought of that, but I was beginning to figure things out a little. "Remember the gold tiepin that turned up tonight? The one the judge lost?"

She nodded.

"Well, he didn't lose it in the house, or the backyard, either. Joel found it in the woods near the summerhouse! Or maybe I should say Animal did, because it was in some junk he found."

Lucy threw her brush on the bed, "Wonder what the old clown was doing down there? He must have been looking for that diary." She frowned. "What do you suppose is in it?"

"I don't know, but it must be important. I just hope we find it first."

I was almost asleep when Lucy nudged me with her elbow. "That was Aunt Matilda laughing downstairs tonight, wasn't it?"

"Had to be," I mumbled sleepily. "Sure wasn't me."

"Creepy, wasn't it? It sounded like it came from every-where and nowhere. . . ."

I didn't say anything. I went to sleep. I was still asleep when she poked me again. "Somebody's at the door," she hissed. She pulled the covers over her head and burrowed down to the foot of the bed.

I jerked the covers away. "Get up, you chicken! It's proba-bly nothing but a ghost." I opened the door a few inches and Animal collided into my feet. Rob was standing in the hall in his pajamas. "Listen. Don't you hear it?" His voice came out in a squeak.

"Hear what?" I yawned.

Lucy stuck her head out from under the covers. "Shhh! I do hear something!"

I held Animal away from the cat and pulled Rob into the room. "It's just a radio," I whispered, listening through a crack in the door. "Or maybe somebody left the TV on."

"At three in the morning?" Lucy showed me the time.

I put on my glasses and took a second look at her watch. "Aunt Matilda sure keeps strange hours! Let's go see what she wants this time."

But Animal had plans of his own. He jumped from my arms and cowered under the bed until Rob fished him out and put him back in his room for safekeeping. Rover blinked and went back to sleep on my pillow.

"Sounds like a piano," Lucy whispered as we stood at the top of the stairs. "Where's it coming from?"

I listened. The tune was familiar: a "busy" tune that Danny likes to hum when she's dusting or mopping. It makes the work go faster, she says.

Rob recognized it, too, and grinned. "She's playing for you, Peg."

Then I remembered the name of the song. It was "When You and I Were Young, Maggie." Maggie is another nickname for Margaret, but nobody ever calls me that.

We crept slowly down the stairs toward the sound. The piano was in the parlor, but the music danced all around us. The silvery notes dissolved like bubbles, one into another.

Louder and faster the music grew until my feet began to tap. We marched downstairs to the happy beat of "Alexander's Ragtime Band" and waited politely for the music to stop. I didn't know whether to clap or not. Are you supposed to applaud for ghosts? Somehow I felt not.

From the big piano in the corner, the last chords rippled and faded into the night. I couldn't see Aunt Matilda, yet I knew she was there. I felt it in the current of cold and the scent that came with it. When I finally did see her, I realized she was different, more transparent than she had been the other times. She was filmy and it scared me. Was Aunt Matilda going away?

"Here we are, Aunt Matilda," I whispered. "We know about Calvin now. We know what you want, but what can we do?"

She moved toward a cupboard in the wall below some bookshelves. I couldn't really see her face, but I could see her eyes—those wide, sad-sparkly eyes were telling us to hurry!

It was an old cupboard. I guess it had been there as long as the house because it was built into the parlor wall. It was small and out-of-the-way, and I don't think Danny had gotten around to cleaning it yet.

Aunt Matilda stood by the spot until she was sure we knew what she wanted. Then she drifted aside while I tugged at the smooth wooden knob until the old walnut door squeaked open.

Inside were a few books and papers and a couple of dusty vases, and it didn't take long for us to see what we were expected to find. Uncle Zeb's diary was right on top!

CHAPTER 20

"That must be what the judge is looking for!" Rob whispered over my shoulder. He quivered as he turned to Aunt Matilda. "What's so important about that diary? What do you want us to do?" But Aunt Matilda was slowly fading away.

"Don't go yet!" Rob begged. "Tell us where to look for the lost invention! Can't you help us find it?"

A light came on at the top of the stairs, and I heard Mama's slippers flopping on the landing. "Uh-oh," I said.

"What on earth are you three doing down here at this time of night? Get back to bed right now!" Mama was sleepy, and when she was sleepy, she's not exactly in the running for "Miss Congeniality."

I crammed the diary back in the cupboard and closed the door. "We'll get it in the morning," I murmured to the others as we were herded upstairs.

But I had forgotten about Sunday school and Danny's book club meeting in the parlor.

We overslept, of course. Rob had already eased Animal outside on the Lazy Day Manual Rotary Machine and was going down to breakfast when we met him on the stairs. Danny was waiting in the kitchen. "There are doughnuts in the breadbox, and you know where to find the cereal," she said. "And hurry, now, or you'll be late for Sunday school."

She shook a wet head of lettuce in the sink and left it to drain while she darted from kitchen to dining room to parlor, and back to the kitchen again, flipping at imaginary crumbs with a dust rag.

We shoveled cereal into our mouths while keeping an eye on the parlor. If only Danny would settle in one place, one of us could—

"Don't dawdle!" Danny snatched away my empty juice glass. "*Tempus fugit!*" (That means "time flies.") "You're going to be late."

"Haste makes waste," I said sweetly, but we got dressed and went to Sunday school. You don't argue with Danny—not much, anyway.

We sat with Mama during church, but Danny didn't come. I wondered if she had been hit by a truck or something, because Danny thinks the church can't get its message across unless she's there to help it along a little . . . I don't guess she ever thought about how God managed before she was born.

"Your grandmother's having her book club over for lunch today," Mama explained as we walked back to Walnut Hill, "so make yourselves scarce, please."

Rob groaned. "Oh, no, not company again! What's gotten into Danny? She must be in a party mood."

Mama laughed. "No, it just happens to be her time to entertain, and she wants to get it out of the way. I don't think they usually meet on Sundays," she said, "but the house was clean, and we had to cook anyway, so she decided to go on and have it today."

We could hear the ladies buzzing before we turned in the front gate, and more were swarming up the walk. The parlor was packed with them: fat ladies, skinny ladies, old ladies, young ladies, and one timid, nervous-looking man.

"Now for goodness' sake, keep those animals out of the parlor!" Mama whispered as we stepped into the hall.

Rob pointed to the lonesome-looking man. "Who's that?"

Danny jerked us into the kitchen. "You know better than

to point! That's Professor Treadwell from the college. He's here to start us off with *The Canterbury Tales.* My book club is studying Chaucer."

Rob giggled. "He sure does look jumpy. You better keep an eye on him, Danny, he might sneak out the window!"

Danny laughed. "Well, I wouldn't blame him, would you?" She folded her hands under her chin in a praying position. "Keep away from the parlor . . . please? And that goes for your menagerie," she added as she swept into the dining room.

I smeared a piece of bread with peanut butter. "How are we going to get that diary out now?"

"How long does the book club last?" Lucy asked.

"Beats me." I shrugged. "We've never had it before."

Lucy helped herself to some of Danny's chicken salad in a cup of crisp lettuce. "Mmmm, if they get to eat this every time, I might even join it myself!"

Rob had all of his fingers covered with carrot curls and was gnawing them off. "Well, I'm not going in there with all those women for all the diaries in the world! We'll just have to wait till it's over."

We had a long wait.

We were still sitting at the table when Joel wandered in. He grabbed the last two cheese straws and attached himself to a chair. "What happened last night after we left? Did you find out anything?"

"I'll say we did!" Rob yelled. "And we could find out something more if we could only get to it."

We told him about the ghostly concert and the diary which was still in the wall cupboard.

Joel opened the kitchen door just a crack, and Professor Treadwell's monotonous voice droned over the clinking of silver forks against Danny's luncheon china. "I sure would like to get my hands on that diary," Joel said.

Lucy listened for a minute. "He's just getting started, so forget it! He spoke to my English class last year and half the class went to sleep."

Joel made a face. "Well, we might as well get started on the next edition of *The Leader*. Who's ready?"

Nobody was, but we started anyway—all except Rob. He wandered in and out like a cat without a corner. Finally, after he had been gone longer than usual, I got suspicious and went after him. I found him outside, lying on his stomach under the parlor window, having a laughing fit! I clamped my hand over his mouth and shoved him into the kitchen. He bit me.

"What's the matter with him?" Joel asked, staring at Rob's red face.

I was wondering if I ought to get a rabies shot. I pushed my brother into a kitchen chair—hard. "That's what I'd like to know," I said. "What were you doing under that window?"

"Watching. . . ." Rob clutched his side and went into another uncontrollable fit. "Just watching Mrs. Moody's nose! It wiggles when she eats!" He gave us a demonstration. "Sometimes it wiggles sideways, like this . . . and sometimes it jumps up and down! Wanna see it? I don't think she's through with her cake yet."

I grabbed him before he got to the door. "Never mind Mrs. Moody's nose! I have a better idea." I whispered in Lucy's ear.

She looked up from the notes she was scribbling. "Now, wait a minute!"

"Sure, why not?" I asked.

"You want me to play the violin *now*?"

I grinned. "I hate to deprive anyone of hearing you play, Lucy. You wouldn't want to neglect Danny's book club, would you?"

"Hey! Neat!" Rob agreed. "Play the one you were practicing the other day: the one with all the squeaks in it."

"Which one? All my songs have squeaks."

"Good," Joel said. "Then it shouldn't take long to evacuate the entire book club. Start screeching!"

Lucy practiced for twenty minutes. The book club vanished in fifteen. "I knew your great talent would come in handy some day," I told her.

But our victory was short-lived. We got rid of one problem . . . along came another. We were helping Mama and Danny clear the clutter from the parlor, trying not to seem too anxious to get them out of the room, when Rob saw the judge coming up the walk with a box under his arm.

Joel watched the judge puff up the steps, and he made a rude noise. "Grab it quick," he whispered, "before he gets inside."

I lunged for the cupboard, snatched the book, and stuck it up the back of my skirt just as Danny opened the front door.

"Why, good afternoon, Judge," Danny said. "What a pleasant surprise." I grinned at Rob. Danny was using her sugar-coated, make-believe voice. What she was really thinking of was all of those unwashed dishes in the sink, and I knew it; the judge didn't, though, so he chugged right on in.

"Just a small token of my appreciation," he said, handing Danny a square, paper-wrapped box. It looked and smelled like what I hoped it was—candy. Danny slipped the box from its wrapper.

"Now, here are some youngsters who might like some chocolates," the judge beamed. "We can't let your grandmother eat them all."

I can't stand being called a *youngster*, and Danny is allergic to chocolate. "By all means," she said, passing the box to Lucy. "Take them back in the kitchen with you, but don't eat too many."

We scrambled down the hall as fast as we could, Lucy with the chocolates and me with my square-looking bottom. I was dying to get a good look at the diary.

Mama was loading the dishwasher; I felt kind of guilty. "Need any help? I asked.

She rescued the candy. "Yes, clear out of here! You've been hanging around like a pack of vultures all day. What's the matter with you?"

We swarmed through the kitchen and crowded out the back door. "I've been watching Mrs. Moody's nose," Rob said.

We went out on the back steps. When I looked back, Mama was still staring at him.

The diary was one of those fat brown ones with a gold clasp. It even had a keyhole, but it wasn't locked.

"It looks like one of those five-year things," Lucy said. "If we have to read through all that, we'll never get through."

But the diary was only half-filled. Uncle Zeb must have started it the year after Aunt Jane died. The first entry said: "The beginning of new year; my first without Jane—not a happy prospect."

Sometimes several days would go by with no written record; maybe nothing happened, or maybe Uncle Zeb just didn't have time to write it down. Most of the entries were about everyday things. He was still practicing medicine, but not as much. He sounded tired.

Joel could read faster than the rest of us. He flipped through the pages, catching a significant word here and there. "Sure did do a lot of fishing," Joel mumbled, "but he never caught much . . . and music, he liked music. Listen to this: 'Went to a concert at the college tonight. The soloist was flat.'" Joel laughed. "Your Uncle Zeb was a music critic!"

Lucy was looking over his shoulder. "Wait a minute!" She poked a finger on the page. "Isn't that the judge's father?"

Joel read the entry aloud: "'Art Hardigree came in today. He's losing to cancer and he knows it. The specialist has returned him to me; there's nothing more he can do—nor can I. Doubt if he makes it past Christmas.'"

"He must mean Arthur Hardigree, Calvin's brother," I said. "Anything else?"

Joel read on. "Not about that. He says Thomas wants him to live with him in Atlanta. Can you imagine the old doctor up there?"

Rob shook his head. "He didn't go, did he?"

"Of course not," Joel answered. "It says right here: 'My patients need me—the few who remain—and I need them as well.'"

"Good for him," I said.

"Good for whom?"

I looked over my shoulder. The judge was standing behind me!

"Why . . . uh . . . good for Joel," I stammered. "He made three runs in yesterday's game at the park!"

Joel slid the book to me and I maneuvered it under the folds of my skirt. For once I was glad my mother made me wear dresses to Sunday school!

"That must be an interesting book." The judge pretended to laugh.

I looked in his eyes. His eyes weren't laughing. "What book?" I lied.

"Why, Judge Hardigree," Joel broke in, "haven't you ever read a naughty book out behind the barn?" He raised one eyebrow in what was supposed to have been a leer. I tried to look guilty.

The judge looked at him for a minute, probably trying to think of something to say. Finally he cleared his throat. "If you happen to run across that diary, I'll make it worth your while."

Rob looked up into his face. "Why? What's so special about that diary?"

The judge looked kind of shook-up. "Well, to tell you the truth, I'm compiling a little history of King's Creek. I expect your uncle's diary to be of enormous help." He mopped his red face.

"I'll bet," I said under my breath.

We waited until he had gone back inside before I slipped the diary out again. I squinted through the screen door. The judge was in the kitchen, getting in Danny's way. "Let's read this down at the summerhouse," I said.

It was quiet in the summerhouse, almost too quiet. I felt like the trees were bending down to listen. It was hot and the dust made me sneeze, but nobody could see us there.

"There's something in here that the judge doesn't want us to find." Joel was staring hard at the open diary.

Lucy was trying to find a seat with no splinters. "Yeah, we got that message." She finally picked a spot. "Wonder what it is?"

Joel was studying the pages. "Uncle Zeb must have known something: something about him or his family that would hurt his chances in politics . . . but what?"

"Maybe he's a vampire," my silly brother said.

"Nyah," I said. "Whoever heard of a fat vampire?"

"He's definitely more the Wolf Man type," Lucy decided. "Have you ever noticed all the hair on the backs of his hands?"

Joel shook his head. "If you three will shut up, we might find the real reason!"

Page by page we thumbed through the book, and somewhere near the middle we found it.

CHAPTER 21

"Having given serious thought to the confession I heard today," Uncle Zeb had written, "I have decided to remain silent. To make an issue of things now would reopen old wounds and hurt innocent people. If only Matilda had known then what I learned today! I hope she understands, wherever she is, that my silence is for kindness' sake. I hope she can forgive me."

Joel's finger hesitated on the page. "I wonder if he saw her, too."

Lucy looked up, her eyes solemn. "He could have helped her, but he didn't! She must have felt it was hopeless!"

"Shhh!" I was trying to read the rest of the page, but I was so excited the words ran together. "Go on, what else does he say?"

"'Arthur Hardigree died today,'" Joel read. "'They called me to his bedside early this morning, but there was nothing I could do . . . nothing anyone could do. He wanted to talk, he said, about Calvin. Said he had to tell someone.

"'At first I thought he was delirious, but I could see there was nothing to do but let him have his say. When I agreed to listen, he made everyone else leave the room. Then he lay still, exhausted on his pillow, and closed his eyes. "I didn't mean to kill my brother," he said.'"

I held my breath as Joel turned the page.

"'Then Arthur told me how he had gotten into an argument with his brother, Calvin, over banking matters, and had ended it by knocking him over the side of the old rock quarry.'"

"Golly!" Lucy gulped. "Wonder what they were fighting about?"

"Just be patient a minute, will you?" Joel barked. He grabbed up the diary and read on: "'Arthur hadn't meant to kill Calvin, but he had been taking small sums of money from the funds for some time, and Calvin knew it. He said Calvin threatened to expose him if he didn't put the money back; the two of them began to fight, and Calvin fell to his death. It was easy to blame the embezzlement on his late brother, Arthur said. But the poor devil had to live with that guilt the rest of his life!'"

"Poor Calvin," Lucy sighed. "All these years he's laid in that disgraceful grave. Just think how long they've waited!"

Rob was looking at the diary. "Is that all it says?"

Joel glanced through the rest of the pages. "That's all. At least that's all it says about the Hardigrees. I guess your Uncle Zeb wrote it down to get if off his mind and then forgot it."

"Why would they go to the quarry to fight? Why not fight at home?" Rob worried.

"I guess they went up there on purpose so nobody would hear them," I told him. "Remember? Calvin had just come back from that town in Alabama. He probably wanted to get things settled before he left for good."

Joel hadn't seen the letter from Calvin in the scrapbook, so we had to tell him about it. "I guess Calvin thought the farther away he was from his brother, the happier he'd be," he said.

"Yeah, and healthier, too," Rob agreed.

Joel handed me the diary. "Well, what do we do now?"

"I don't know. I guess we'll have to convince Mama or Danny to help us. But right now we're going to have to find a safe place for this diary. The judge knows we have it, and if he tells Mama, she'll make us give it to him."

"I'd like to give it to him," Joel growled. He thought for a minute. "Can you keep it in your room?"

"At night, maybe, as long as I'm around, but during the day nothing's safe from Danny and her dust rag. She'd be sure to find it."

"Well, we'll have to think of someplace. You can't go dragging a diary around with you all the time. That would look suspicious."

"Hey, I think I know a place," I said. "We could keep an eye on it in the daytime, and nobody would even think of looking there!"

"Not the summerhouse," Lucy whispered. "He's already looked here once."

"I know," I nodded. "Remember the day I bumped into him over at the college and asked him about Aunt Matilda? Well, he must have thought I knew something. Maybe he thought I had already read the diary. I think he came out here to look for it."

"And lost his tiepin," Rob added.

"That's right, and he was snooping around again while we were working on *The Leader*. That was no dog that scattered the box of news stories!" I made a face at Joel.

He shrugged. "Well? What other spot do you have in mind?"

I looked around before I answered. It would take a fat tree to hide the judge, but you never can tell. "The toolbox on the back porch," I told them. "Nobody ever uses it, and it's convenient."

"You mean that heavy wooden box under the kitchen window?" Joel asked.

I nodded. "Even if we couldn't watch it all the time, it's close enough to the house to be safe, and I can keep the diary in my room at night."

"I think you're right," Joel agreed. He even smiled. Maybe he was trying to make up for not believing me about the box of scattered news articles. Whatever the reason, I liked it.

CHAPTER 22

We found a good hiding place for the diary that night in the puzzle box with Aunt Matilda's scrapbook. On top of that we stacked five comic books, a Monopoly game, and a papier-mâché panda I made in the fifth grade. It looked naturally messy. Then Lucy and I settled down to the serious business of painting our toenails.

Lucy yawned and I found myself yawning, too. It was late and we were supposed to have been in bed, but after all, it was the last night of her visit.

We took time about smearing our nails with "Metallic Sunset." It looked like our feet were on fire.

"Something bothers me about the judge," Lucy decided, trying to rub the sunset glow from her fingers.

"A lot of things bother me about the judge," I said. "And yet I can't help feeling sorry for him in a way. He shouldn't be blamed for what his father did. It wasn't his fault."

"That's what bothers me. How does he know what his father did?"

"I don't know. I guess I never thought about it. Maybe his father told him."

"I don't think so," Lucy said. "Would you tell your own son you killed somebody?"

"No, I don't guess so."

"And besides," she added, "how did he know about your uncle's diary? He had to find out from somewhere that your Uncle Zeb knew about the murder."

"Maybe Uncle Zeb told him, or he could have been listening when his father was dying. He might have heard him confess. Besides, almost everybody knew Uncle Zeb kept a diary."

I stretched to keep from yawning again, but it didn't help. "I just wish he'd leave us alone about it," I said. "Nobody wants to hurt him. All I want to do is make Aunt Matilda happy."

Lucy jumped as the door creaked open. "Oh, it's you!" Rob poked his head in the room.

"There's such a thing as knocking," I reminded him.

"I can't find Animal," he moaned. "I even threw a leftover hamburger in the basket, but he didn't come!"

Lucy put her arm around him. (He would have socked *me* for that.) "Don't worry, Robert," she said. "Animal's around here somewhere. He's probably just exploring."

"Did you whistle?" I asked.

"I was afraid to whistle any louder. Danny might hear. I've been calling for ages. He just isn't here!"

"You don't suppose he went back to Joel's, do you?" Lucy suggested. "Maybe he misses his mother."

"No, I don't think so," I said. "Not after this long." I laughed, trying to make Rob smile. "Maybe Animal went to *his* book club. They're reading *The Hound of the Baskervilles*, you know."

But Rob didn't think it was funny. He was really worried. And when Animal didn't show up for breakfast, I began to worry too. So did Danny, but she tried not to show it.

Rob called Joel before we even sat down to breakfast, but Animal hadn't turned up there. Joel promised to drop by to help us look after he finished working at Miss Ida's.

"Oh, he'll turn up way before then!" I said. But after we had combed the neighborhood, even I began to have doubts.

Robert's face was getting longer and longer. Even Danny

couldn't calm him down. He flitted from one place to another, his face getting redder and his voice getting louder.

Danny tried to reason with him. "Try not to think about him," she said. "Just forget about it for a little while and he'll come back. A watched pot never boils!" But I heard her whispering over the phone to some of her friends who lived near the college. None of them had seen a fuzzy, flop-eared dog. "We'll find him," Danny promised, "if we have to put an ad in the paper."

Mama called from the store about mid-morning to see if Animal had turned up, and Rob talked with her a long time over the phone. When he hung up he wasn't as jumpy. I guess Mama must know some magic words.

But they weren't magic enough to bring Animal back. We sat on the back porch, hoping to see a familiar black-tipped tail zigzagging through the tall grass, straining to hear a happy bark. It was a strange day. The sun was too bright; the leaves were too still. The heat and the silence were screaming at each other. We were going to have a storm. I felt like it was lurking somewhere, watching us, waiting to pounce! And poor, funny little Animal would be out there lost in it.

I heard the phone ring in the house and held my breath, hoping it would be somebody who had seen our puppy. But it was only the library calling to tell Danny that the mystery she wanted had come in.

"Look after your brother for a few minutes, will you, Peggy?" she asked on her way out. "I don't like to leave him right now, but this is the latest book out by my favorite mystery writer. If I don't grab it now, someone else will."

"Mystery!" I hooted. "I thought you were supposed to be studying Chaucer! What will your book club think?"

Danny looked at me as if she wouldn't give two cents for what they thought. "Yours is not to reason why," she said and pulled my bangs. "I'll be right back." She hurried down the walk with an armload of books.

"I wish Joel would come," Rob sighed for the third time that morning. I was getting a little tired of the way he looked up to Joel. He thought Joel was Superman!

I looked at the kitchen clock. It was after eleven. When the telephone rang again, I jumped up to catch it on the first ring. This time it *had* to be good news. *Oh please,* I thought, *let it be about Animal!*

The call was about Animal, but it wasn't good.

"If you want your little dog back," a muffled voice said, "you'd better do just as I say!"

CHAPTER 23

"Did you understand what I said?" snapped the voice at the other end of the line.

I just stood there like a dummy with the telephone glued to my ear. Finally I nodded, then remembered that the caller couldn't see me. "Yes," I squeaked, "I heard you."

The screen door slammed and I turned to see the others standing there staring—staring and listening. Robert started to say something, but I warned him to be quiet.

"Where is he? What did you do with Animal?" I yelled. The numbness had worn off and I was mad, so mad it scared me. I wanted to reach through the telephone and scratch the hateful, unknown face!

"There's an empty garage," the voice began, "in back of the Anderson place. Do you know where that is?"

I glanced at Lucy. "The Anderson Place?" I whispered.

"It's that old ruin on Church Street where the house burned last year. I know where it is."

My cold fingers knotted around the phone. "Yes, I know it." My voice was shaking.

"Be there in ten minutes." There was a final-sounding click and I was listening to the dial tone.

"That was about Animal, wasn't it?" Rob was tugging at my arm.

"Quit it, that hurts!" I jerked my arm away and grabbed the phone book out of the drawer.

"What are you doing?" he shouted. "Who was that? Where's Animal?"

"I'm calling Joel." I flipped through the pages until I found Miss Ida's number. Minnie Bell answered, and after an eternity of explanations and precious minutes of echoing silence, Joel came to the phone.

I tried not to stammer when I told him about the call, but I was scared and mad and worried all at once. My sentences tumbled out upside down.

Joel's voice was cool and steady. "Calm down and start over." I felt better. I took a deep breath and told him what the man had said.

"Don't do anything until I get there!" he warned me. "It could be some kind of a trap; it might be dangerous!"

"But Animal—"

"Never mind! I'll be right over. Now stay there!"

Rob had been listening to my part of the conversation. He turned and ran for the kitchen door. Lucy went after him.

"No, wait!" I called. "Joel said not to do anything until he gets here!"

Rob didn't look back. "But the man said *ten minutes*! We have to get there in ten minutes!"

Lucy looked from Robert to me and then started after him. "I don't think we should wait either," she said. "Something might happen!" The two of them raced across the porch and disappeared around the side of the house.

I stumbled down the back steps and yelled for them to stop, but they didn't. I didn't know what to do. I couldn't let my little brother walk into some kind of trap while I waited there for Joel.

The others had gone. I stared into an empty yard. I would have to take a shortcut to catch up with them now. The old, burned Anderson house was only a few blocks away. Joel would know where we had gone.

I cut across the back lot, jumping a low border of iris,

where the mowed end of the lawn collided with the trees, and fell flat on my face!

I picked myself up off the ground and straightened my glasses. It was almost as if a foot had tripped me. I examined the spot where I had fallen. There was no sign of a root, not even a medium-sized rock. Feeling clumsier than usual, I brushed the pine straw from my jeans and charged ahead. It was like walking into a brick wall—something pushed me back again.

I staggered backward and sat on the ground. How could I walk into a tree when a tree wasn't there? Even *I* could see better than that. Then I heard the dry rustle of her skirt and sniffed the stale, woodsy smell. Finally I got Aunt Matilda's message! I looked around. I couldn't see her, but her presence was there; I could feel it in the air. Aunt Matilda's cold vapors stirred past me. Something was going to happen. . . .

A slight, hot breeze ruffled the leaves behind me and I looked up to see dark, mean-looking clouds hanging low in the sky. I felt a sense of urgency, a frantic impulse to do something—anything! I found myself running toward the back porch . . . toward the toolbox where we had hidden Uncle Zeb's diary that morning. Then I knew what Aunt Matilda wanted me to do: I had to hide that diary, and quickly. But where?

I rummaged in the box for the book and grabbed it. But what now? My face was wet with sweat and my hair was sticking to my forehead in soppy ringlets. I felt trapped, like a fugitive with nowhere to go!

Then I saw the basement door. It was the best I could do; I was inside in a second. The dark and cold of the basement felt good after the heat of the sun. I looked around; there were dark corners, boxes, and rows of shelves: lots of places to hide.

I stopped just long enough to unscrew the light bulb from the overhead socket, then hurried to the darkest corner and crawled behind an old filing cabinet. The hard earth floor was cold and damp; I could feel it through my jeans. My breathing was frantic and loud. It made the basement sound like an echo chamber.

Will you cool it? I told myself. *Just calm down. He won't look here. He can't look here!*

Then there was the faintest creak of the door and a glimpse of light—but only for a minute. Someone was there in the room—somewhere in the basement with me.

I shut my eyes tight and told God if He would get me out of this one, I'd never hit my brother again . . . I'd make my bed neatly every day . . . even clean the ring from the bathtub. I wondered if He would still believe me; I had promised before.

I covered my mouth to still my breathing. It was black dark in my corner and I didn't dare to look, but I heard his footsteps: soft, deliberate footsteps coming nearer. His breathing was short, as if he were out of breath. It sounded like he was right on top of me.

"Peggy?" His voice was a whisper. "I'll have that diary now, please."

I scrunched up in my corner and died a thousand times. I would have to run past him; that was my only chance! He was well past middle age, but he was still stronger than I was—maybe smarter, too. Besides, I was afraid of him. I don't think he was afraid of me.

He bumped his head on an overhanging pipe and said something my mother wouldn't want me to hear. In that moment I dodged past him toward the door, toward freedom!

As usual, gracefulness avoided me. My foot hit something that rolled. I had forgotten about the light bulb! Crack! It gave way under me and I went flying one way, the diary another.

I landed, stunned, on my stomach against the brick wall. He had the diary before I could get to my feet. I heard him running for the door.

I felt like crying; my shoulder hurt where I had hit the wall, and the arm was bent on my glasses. "Oh, stop! Please don't take that," I begged. But I knew he wouldn't listen. He was gone.

The door was open and I popped out of that basement like

a rocket being launched. Even the stormy skies looked good to me. I took a deep breath of that good ol' hot, soggy air and took out after the judge. I knew it was the judge. For the first time I noticed his dark raincoat with a hat pulled low over his ears . . . some disguise!

Don't ever believe it if anybody tells you that fat people can't run. The judge was barreling across the backyard like Hank Aaron coming in home!

"Stop!" I screamed, holding my bruised shoulder. "Give it back, it's not yours!" But for all my yelling, he was getting away.

Then something funny happened; funny *strange*, not funny *ha-ha* . . . well, really it was both. The judge took a flying dive, as if he had tripped over an invisible wire, and landed on his hands and knees, rocking back and forth like a crawling baby!

I heard a ferocious growl and saw a speeding blur of brown race across the yard. It was Animal! He went for the judge's ankle and hung on! At the same time, Joel came tearing around the house from the front.

"Grab him, Joel!" I yelled. "He has the diary!" Animal was still snacking on the judge's shoe.

"Get that mongrel off of me!" Judge Hardigree bellowed. "That dog must be mad!"

I took Animal by the collar and dragged him away, still growling. I tied him to the porch with a piece of rope, and from the way he was snapping at the judge, it's a good thing I did.

"You ought to have that animal put to sleep!" the judge snarled. "It's vicious!" His bulbous nose was glowing and there were tears in his eyes. I don't know if he was crying because he was hurt or just plain mad, but I did know the judge had reached his limit. We were on dangerous ground. He picked up his hat, stuck the diary under his arm, and started to walk away.

That doesn't belong to you, Judge Hardigree," I said. He ignored me.

"Haven't you done enough?" I asked. "You kidnapped our dog and scared us half to death! That's my Uncle Zeb's diary. It doesn't belong to you."

He turned, and I didn't like the look he gave me. "Your uncle wanted me to have this diary," he puffed, "and I'm going to take it."

"We already know about the murder, Judge," Joel said in a low, steady voice. "You don't have to cover up for that. It wasn't your fault."

The judge turned purple! He made a furious lunge for Joel, but Joel was too quick. It was like trying to grab a bar of soap with wet hands.

"Peggy, are you all right? What's going on here?" It was Danny. I don't remember having seen Danny run before, but she was running then, scattering library books like stepping stones on the grass.

Judge Hardigree was trying to recover his dignity. He mumbled something about a misunderstanding and hid the diary under his raincoat.

"Why, Judge Hardigree, what are you doing here?" Danny sounded suspicious. "Is anything wrong?"

He straightened his collar. "Well—yes, you might say something's wrong! Your granddaughter here has insulted me, and her vicious dog has attacked me. Something is most definitely wrong, madam!"

"Danny, don't believe him!" I shouted. "He kidnapped Animal and put him in a garage somewhere. Then, when he had us good and worried, he called and told us where to find him so we'd be gone when he came to get the diary! Only I fooled him! I stayed behind."

Lucy and Rob came racing across the yard about then, redfaced and out of breath.

"Where's Animal?" Rob yelled. "He ran off and left us."

Joel pointed to the puppy, still yelping at the end of his leash. "You missed all the excitement," he said.

Danny was staring at the judge. "I don't understand. What's so important about that diary?"

Joel flushed under the judge's threatening look, but he told her anyway.

Danny opened her mouth and closed it again. "Well, I don't see how you think that could hurt you, Judge. You didn't kill your uncle! I hope you didn't think we would hold that against you."

"You're not in politics, Mrs. Summerville," the judge sighed.

"He has the diary under his raincoat, Danny," I said. "Ask him how he got it!"

Danny looked at the judge and the judge looked at Danny. Each was waiting for the other to make the first move. "Were you the one who telephoned me about the library book?" Danny asked finally.

The judge didn't say anything.

Danny's eyes snapped. "I walked all the way there before I remembered that the library is closed on Monday mornings. You did that to get me out of the house, didn't you?"

Just then the diary under the judge's raincoat slid to the ground and he made a move to grab it. His chubby fingers came within an inch of it, but the book slid out of his reach! Again he clutched at it, and again, but it kept slipping away. He ended up with only a fistful of grass.

The sun disappeared as if somebody had turned off the light, and the first raindrops spattered from the sky. Aunt Matilda began to laugh. Have you ever wondered what lilies of the valley would sound like if they could ring? Well, Aunt Matilda's laugh was like that, soft and silvery. Then, as the rain fell harder, the laughter got louder until it was all around us—like the rain.

The judge knelt in the wet grass over the fallen book and covered his ears until the last whisper of haunting laughter died away.

"By the way, Judge Hardigree," I said, "I don't believe you've met my Great-Aunt Matilda!"

CHAPTER 24

Danny leaned over and picked up the diary. It lay still in her hands. The judge looked like he was falling apart. "I'm going to have to sit down," he said.

Danny led him to the porch. "We're all getting wet. Do you want to come inside?"

He shook his head and squashed down into a straight chair on the back porch. For a minute he just sat there, wet and limp and old. His eyes weren't threatening anymore. They were nothing—just blank. "That book will ruin me," he mumbled, pulling his raincoat closer about him.

"No, Judge," Danny said, "You'll ruin yourself. No one could have blamed you for something your father did before you were born . . . but what you did today, I *do* blame you for that."

I stared down at his vacant face. "Judge Hardigree . . . how did you know your father kil— Er . . . how did you know your father did what he did?"

His expression didn't change. I thought he was never going to answer, but he did. "I always suspected something, I guess, from the way my father acted whenever his brother's name was mentioned. And it got worse as he grew older. There was an intercom by his bed with a speaker in my room next door, so I could hear him in the night." He shivered slightly. "The switch was on—as usual—I just slipped into my room and listened." The judge looked at Danny. "I had to know."

Danny shook her head. "It would have been so much better if you hadn't. If you hadn't been so anxious to get that diary, the children might never have read it."

"Oh, yes we would!" I said, thinking of Aunt Matilda. "But how could you be sure Uncle Zeb even mentioned your father's secret in his diary?"

The judge shifted in his chair. "Because I read it. I came to see Zeb once just before he died; he was dozing and the diary was on the bedside table. I was going to tear the pages out, but just then the nurse came in and I had to leave. I can't tell you how it has haunted me! Can't you see? I *had* to destroy it . . . at all costs . . . I *had* to!"

Danny looked down at Animal snoozing under the porch. "That dog isn't vicious, Judge Hardigree; you're the one who is vicious."

He shrugged. "What do you want me to do?"

Danny looked at me and smiled. "I don't care what you do," she said, "but I think someone else does."

He shuddered. "Do you mean that horrible thing that laughs? What does it want with me?"

"Aunt Matilda isn't horrible," I protested. "She's just tired—tired of waiting. Move Calvin into the cemetery," I begged him. "That's all she wants!"

His face was gray. "Then will she leave me alone? Will you leave me alone?"

"I think she'll be happy then," I said.

The judge stared at the tips of his pink fingers. "All right," he agreed finally. "I'll make necessary arrangements tomorrow. But it will be a day or so before they'll be able to move the body."

"She'll want him to have a funeral," I reminded him. "With a minister and everything."

For a minute I thought he would argue, but he didn't. He only grunted as he made his way carefully down the steps and into the summer rain.

"I hope you realize what this is going to cost me," he growled.

"Judge Hardigree," I called after him, "don't worry about the diary! We'll destroy it, I promise."

But I don't think he even heard me.

Danny stared after the judge plodding away through the drizzle. "He's going to get soaking wet," she said. But she didn't seem too sorry about it.

I took her hand as we went inside. "Danny," I began, "I hope you weren't . . . I mean, you and the judge. . . ."

Danny squeezed my hand and laughed. "I might be old, Peggy Patrick, but I'm not desperate! I hope you give me credit for more sense than that."

Soon the kettle was steaming and we drank hot tea with our sandwiches at the big kitchen table. It was way past noon, but nobody was very hungry, except Animal. He wallowed in puppy happiness under the kitchen table and gobbled up all of his lunch—and most of ours.

Danny carried her second cup of tea into the parlor and sank into the big chair by the window. "Don't you think it's time you told me about our ghost?" she said.

Of course everybody wanted to talk at once, but we finally pieced everything together in kind of a patchwork way.

"And you say Ida Whiteside saw her, too?" Danny's eyes were almost as round as the teacup she was holding.

"Twice," Lucy answered.

"Why didn't somebody tell me?"

I grinned. "Would you have believed us?"

"No, I suppose not." She put her half-empty teacup on the table beside her, pushing aside a heavy open book.

"Which of you is reading this old thing?" she asked. "I must have put it back on the shelf three or four times in the last day or so, and someone keeps getting it out again."

"I started reading *Huck Finn*," I said, "but I thought I left it upstairs."

Danny shook her head. "No, this is a musty old history of

the college. I keep finding it here open to the same page."

Joel and I jumped up at the same time. "Let me see that book!" I shouted.

The pages were yellow and brittle with that peculiar stale smell that old books have. It was turned to a photograph of one of the early college buildings. A small man in a beaver hat stood on the steps. Rob stared at the picture. "I've seen that building!" he said.

The small print under the photograph read:

Dr. Joseph Summerville stands on the steps of the old library building where he was said to have experimented with an early form of the electric light.

Lucy was frowning at the photograph. "Why, that's not the library; that's the Literary Hall!"

Rob reached out a grimy paw, but I jerked the book away. "You'll ruin it with those filthy hands!"

He gritted his teeth. "How can you think of dirt at a time like this? What else does it say?"

"There's a whole chapter on Great-Great-Great-Grandfather Summerville. It describes the demonstration and everything. Listen!"

The doctor's room was darkened to simulate night. Over the table in front of his desk was suspended a large glass tube. In this was placed a piece of charcoal connected to wires from an electrical machine near the lecturer. As soon as the electric current was turned on, the carbon began to glow, and finally reached a white heat, emitting a light of dazzling brilliancy. There seems no doubt that this was the first electric light bulb in America, if not in the world.

Everybody was quiet for a minute, but not for long. "Gosh!" I said finally. Rob jumped over the back of the sofa and did a handstand in the middle of the parlor. "We've found it!" he yelled. "We've finally found it!"

Danny took the book out of my hands. "Now, calm down a minute, Robert. We've only found a description of the invention and a picture of the old library where it was. We don't know if it's still there."

Rob wiggled his toes in the air. "It has to be! It just has to be!"

Somehow I knew we would find it then. "It's there," I told him. But I don't know why I said it.

Danny turned the pages carefully. "Why, this old thing's even older than I am. It was published back in 1892!"

The book was brown and a little ragged, and there were spots on the cover, it had been on the shelf so long. "Just think," I said, "it's been right here in this room all along, and we didn't know it!"

Joel was looking a little mixed-up. "But you said you talked with Professor Pittman. He's supposed to be the campus historian. Why didn't he know about this book?"

"Don't forget that most of the old books burned ages ago in that library fire," I reminded him. "This might be the only copy left."

Danny smiled. "That's right. We might have a rare collector's item, although I can't imagine who would want it, except maybe an old college family. I doubt if many were printed to begin with. Probably no one remembers there ever was a history."

"Aunt Matilda remembered," Rob grinned.

Danny nodded sadly. "Poor Matilda! If the judge had escaped with that diary, we would never have proof that her Calvin was innocent."

Lucy frowned. "What I want to know is, how did he know the diary was still around—that it hadn't been thrown away?"

Danny sipped a swallow of cold tea and made a face. "I'm afraid that's my fault. Do you remember the first time he came to see us?"

"When he slipped on the steps?" Rob laughed.

"I'll bet Aunt Matilda did that," I said. "I heard her laugh."

"She was the one who squashed the judge's hat, too," Rob added. He frowned at Danny. "And we got the blame!"

Danny looked embarrassed. "We live and learn," she said. "But I was telling you about the diary: the judge mentioned it the day he came over; asked if I had seen it anywhere. I told him I thought I had when we came here to see Thomas about buying the house, but that I didn't know where it was now."

Rob gulped. "Gosh, Danny, why did you do that?"

Danny shook her head. "How was I to know it was so important? We were talking about Zeb, and he told me what a help he had been when his father died. The judge and I discussed the fact that Zeb kept a diary. It seemed an unusual thing for a busy man to do, and I was wondering how he found the time. That was when the judge said something about Zeb wanting him to have it. Now that I think about it, he did seem a little too anxious."

I looked out the parlor window. The afternoon sun was steaming puddles from the walk, and a light breeze ruffled the open pages of the book on Danny's lap.

"Hey, it's stopped raining!" Rob yelled. "Let's go over to the campus and see what we can find in the Literary Hall."

"Wait a minute," Danny said. "I think it will be easier for you if I make a phone call first."

"It's all right," she told us a few minutes later. "Professor Pittman will meet you in front of the building. I think he's as excited as you are."

I started for the door—then stopped. "Hold on a minute," I said. "There's something I gotta do first!"

Rob stamped his foot. "Like what?"

"Like make my bed," I said.

His mouth fell open. "Make your *bed*? At a time like this?"

I grinned. "Well, I made this promise, you see. . . ."

CHAPTER 25

Finding the lost invention wasn't quite as easy as I thought it was going to be, and for a while I wondered if we were going to find it at all. The downstairs of the Literary Hall was used as meeting rooms for the different honor societies. The upstairs served as an office for the college yearbook. Our search turned up nothing but the usual tables, desks, and filing cabinets. It looked like another dead end.

"Maybe there's a secret room somewhere!" (My brother watches too much television.)

"What about the basement?" I asked. "Could it be down there?"

Joel shook his head. "Not unless your ancestor invented the furnace. That's all there is—I've looked."

"That's not fair!" I stamped my soggy sneaker and a puddle oozed out. "After all this trouble, we still can't find it! I just knew it would be here."

Professor Pittman smiled. "Don't give up yet, my impatient young leh-dy. This is a three-story building. There's still an attic, you know. We have another floor yet to go."

"But there's no way to get up there," I argued, staring at the ceiling over the second floor landing. "And even if there were, how would we get in? There's no door."

The professor laughed in his slow, rustling voice as if he

weren't in a hurry at all. "I'll be willing to bet there's an opening of some kind under this acoustical tile. This ceiling hasn't been here for more than twenty years at the most. They probably had it lowered to economize on the heat."

Joel was grinning. "Those are removable tiles, aren't they? My dad used those in our basement once. They just lift out."

"That's right," the professor agreed, "and if we can get someone with a long enough ladder, we'll find out what's above it."

Well, it took some doing, and we heard a lot of grumbling from the maintenance department, but the professor wasn't taking "no" for an answer. After a while two workmen came over with a long extension ladder. They weren't very happy about it.

One of them was the crabby janitor from the art department. His name was George, we learned, and he was just as grouchy as he had been the first time we met. Maybe even grouchier. He and the other guy exchanged sour looks while the professor figured out where the door might be.

I don't know how the others felt, but I was about ready to jump out of my skin. Professor Pittman was as calm as if he were deciding where to hang a picture—turning his head this way and that, pulling at his beard, and squinting at the ceiling.

"I'm certain the old stairs used to continue to the attic or the third floor," he decided, after pacing the length of the hall. "Your ancestor was too advanced in years to be climbing a ladder to his lab every day. The permanent stairs were probably torn down when they quit using the third story. So . . . if we just follow the turn of the stairs . . . the opening should be just about . . . here." He pointed to a spot above him on the opposite side of the hall. The two workmen snorted a lot, but they finally propped the ladder in place.

I thought they would never finish removing that tile, but after a few jittery minutes of waiting, a dark square hole opened up. They had to use a flashlight to find it, but they finally reached the original ceiling.

"There's some kind of trapdoor up here all right," the first man called down in a hollow voice. "But it may take a crow-bar to open it."

It didn't. After a couple of whacks the door creaked back-ward with a slam, and a pale square of daylight jumped through. It had been waiting a long time.

Professor Pittman stood on tiptoe and peered up the new shaft of light. He wasn't calm anymore. George had stepped carefully onto the third floor. "Whew! It's hot up here!" he shouted.

"Never mind that!" called the professor. "What do you see up there?"

"Nothin'. Just some kind of machine is all."

The professor's beard shook. "Nothing? 'Nothing,' he says! How I would like to climb up there and see that *nothing*! But at my age I suppose it's wiser to wait." He turned to the four of us. "Well, what are you waiting for? Go on up and tell me about it; but be careful where you step!"

George was as anxious to come down as we were to go up. He mopped his red face. "You can have it," he muttered. We scrambled up the ladder, trying not to step on each other's fingers. The heat wrapped itself around us, and the dry musty smell made me sneeze.

The forgotten lab was shrouded in dust, but it was still there. The clumsy electrical machine with its large revolving disc stood in the center of the room like a king on his throne in some forgotten kingdom. The handle still turned that made the disc work against small brushes to create electrical friction. And the strange-looking glass globe hung suspended over Great-Great-Great-Grandfather's empty table where it had been waiting for over a hundred years—waiting for its creator's magic touch.

I felt like I had stepped into a vacuum, like there were no such things as time and war and death.

Rob shoved me aside, knocking my hand from the han-dle. "You're not turning it fast enough! Let me!"

"No!" Joel stopped him. "You'll ruin the whole thing. It's been here too long. It might fall apart. Wait until it can be checked over by somebody who knows what he's doing."

Rob gave him a dirty look, but he left the shaky old machine alone. Later we found out that it did need reinforcing. After that the head of the physics department showed us how it worked—and it did work! The funny light bulb blazed like ten thousand candles, and Rob's eyes were almost as bright. I guess mine were too.

Professor Pittman said that the old inventor probably had the lab closed up after the War Between the States. His health wasn't good and there was no money. People were more interested in keeping alive than they were in electricity. If the war hadn't interrupted his work, he might have gone on to develop his light as others later did. That's something we'll never know.

"But it seems like the college would have at least preserved the lab," Joel said. "I can't understand why they would tear down the stairs and seal it off that way."

"I expect the old stairs became unsafe, or even damaged," the professor explained. "And since no one ever used the third floor, they just did away with them. This little college had barely enough money to keep going in the latter part of the 1800s. They had to economize where they could."

I wondered if the professor's poetry was anything like his speech. It had a rhythm like water flowing—cool, gentle water just taking its time. "I wonder now," he went on, his voice fainter, "did the old inventor know his work was finished? Does he care that we've brought it to light again?"

Suddenly he smiled at Rob and me. "I think he knows what we've done; somehow I feel he has known all along . . . and I believe he's glad. Don't you?"

I nodded. I thought so, too, but just then I couldn't say a word.

It was an exciting day a few months later when the college reopened the little lab as a museum. Rob and I got to snip the ribbon at the dedication ceremony. I don't know who was prouder, Rob or the professor, when we walked up those brand new stairs for the first time. But it wasn't nearly as exciting as that strange, steaming day in August when we discovered the attic's secret.

As for Judge Arthur P. Hardigree, he decided to drop out of the political race after Calvin's unusual funeral. I guess he was ashamed to run for office after the way he behaved about the diary. (We burned that, of course.) Anyway, he doesn't come to see us anymore, and that's a relief!

I never thought I would enjoy a funeral, but Calvin's was different. The judge didn't come, but he sent a pretty spray of red carnations—and for Judge Hardigree, that's at least a step in the right direction.

Miss Ida was there—and without Minnie Bell—with the last of her summer pinks, and Lucy brought chrysanthemums, a great big armload of fluffy white ones.

We didn't have a flower in bloom in our whole yard, but Danny helped us to make an evergreen wreath of magnolia leaves and cedar. She said that the wreath was symbolic of everlasting life; somehow I thought that made it right.

There were only eight of us there, counting all of my family, plus Joel, Lucy, and of course Miss Ida and the minister.

The services were short, but it was enough. For music, Joel played "Greensleeves" on his guitar. It's not something you'd hear at the usual funeral, I guess. But then this wasn't the usual funeral. The notes rang sweet and clear over the shady old graveyard that summer afternoon. It made me feel peaceful inside.

As Joel strummed his song, we stooped and placed our flowers on the fresh mound. Everyone was strangely quiet as he sang the beautiful words:

> *I have been ready at thy hand*
> *To grant whatever thou would crave.*
> *I have waged both life and land,*
> *Thy love and goodwill for to have. . . .*

I heard a sigh, as soft as a leaf rustling in the willows, as light as the whisper of midnight snow. And the scent of sweet, fresh roses surrounded us and then was gone.

But there weren't any roses there.